DISCOVER

READ

EXPLORE

LEARN

**NEW HANOVER COUNTY
PUBLIC LIBRARY**

# famous
# in a
# small
# town

Henry Holt and Company • New York

# famous

# in a

# small

# town

# emma mills

Henry Holt and Company, *Publishers since 1866*
Henry Holt® is a registered trademark of Macmillan Publishing Group, LLC
175 Fifth Avenue, New York, NY 10010 • fiercereads.com

Library of Congress Control Number: 2018945021
ISBN 978-1-250-17963-0

Our books may be purchased in bulk for promotional, educational, or business use. Please
contact your local bookseller or the Macmillan Corporate and Premium Sales Department
at (800) 221-7945 ext. 5442 or by e-mail at MacmillanSpecialMarkets@macmillan.com.

First edition, 2019 / Designed by Liz Dresner
Printed in the United States of America
1 3 5 7 9 10 8 6 4 2

*Becky—this is me dedicating a book to you*

I'm not trying to make this a downer, understand. I mean, I really do think that love is the best thing in the world, except for cough drops. But I also have to say, for the umpty-umpth time, that life isn't fair. It's just fairer than death, that's all.

—WILLIAM GOLDMAN, *The Princess Bride*

*Getting smaller in the rearview*
*Sitting taller as I drive*
*Lord help me, I'm never going back*
*Lord help me, but I am never ever going back*

—MEGAN PLEASANT, "Steel Highway"

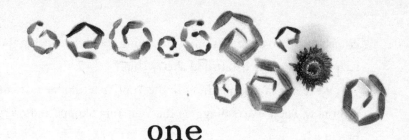

# one

Brit had been fired from the Yum Yum Shoppe, which came as a shock to approximately no one.

We sat on top of one of the picnic tables outside McDonald's afterward, eating vanilla cones in defiance. The sun had set, but the sky still had that pinky-blueness to it, fading to purple as we cursed Brit's manager, the Yum Yum Shoppe, its fourteen flavors of ice cream, and every person who asks for more than two samples while there's a line.

"No, screw that," Brit said. "People who ask for samples in general. There are fourteen flavors. There have been fourteen flavors there for the last, like, *fifty-seven years*. Really? You want to sample strawberry? Do you really need to *try* strawberry?"

"In the Yum Yum Shoppe's defense, there were twelve flavors up until, like, five years ago. Remember, they added peanut butter

crunch, but then there was this whole thing about there being thirteen flavors so they had to add cherry chip?"

"We're not saying anything in the Yum Yum Shoppe's defense right now, Soph. We're dragging the Yum Yum Shoppe and everyone in it."

"I'll never go there again," I said, even though I knew I would.

"Thank you," Brit replied, even though she knew it too.

The truth was, if I stopped going to places just because Brit got fired from them, I couldn't go very many places. It's a testament to how small our town was, and also how often Brit cycled through jobs.

"It's fine," she said, in that way where I knew it really wasn't fine, but she wanted to believe it was. "What do I want to spend all summer scooping ice cream for anyway? I'd end up with one jacked arm and one puny arm. Who needs that in their life?" She gestured with her cone. "All they have to do to make one of these is pull a stupid lever."

"I'll ask Mel if there's something at the library," I said, chasing a dribbler running down the side of my cone. It was hot out, and the soft serve was melting fast.

"You don't have to do that."

"No, just come by on Monday."

"I can get another job all by myself, Sophie."

*And you can get yourself fired from it too.* "I know."

We finished up our ice cream in silence. Brit leaned back on the tabletop when she was done, folding her arms behind her head. She was still wearing her Yum Yum Shoppe T-shirt, an anthropomorphic ice cream cone on the front with FOURTEEN FLAVORS OF FUN printed in big bubble letters around it. The cone itself was flashing a double thumbs-up and a crazed smile. Its eyes seemed to say, *Try the strawberry, you know you fucking want to.*

"Okay," Brit said, and I knew a question was coming. "What do you want right now?"

"I mean, I would like it if the deranged Yum Yum Shoppe cone wasn't staring at me."

"I'm going to burn this shirt."

"Good."

"In the fire pit. Tonight. With extra lighter fluid."

"You should."

"It's gonna be a literal tower of flames."

"We'll dance around it."

Brit glanced over at me. "Will you drop it off for me tomorrow, though? Tyler said he'd take it out of my paycheck if I didn't bring it back."

"You want me to give Tyler the ashes?"

She grinned. "I probably like the idea of burning it better than I'd like the actual burning of it."

"It's good you know that about yourself."

It was quiet for a moment, her grin fading in contemplation. "For real, though. What do you want right now? If you could have the one thing you want most in the world, right this second, what would it be?"

Sometimes Brit's questions were a joke. Sometimes they were a test. You couldn't laugh at them in case it was the latter, and if indeed it was, you'd never know for sure if you'd passed or not, except for the slight wrinkle that occasionally appeared between her eyebrows that meant you probably answered wrong.

"For everyone I love to get everything they want," I said.

In this case, the wrinkle appeared immediately. "That's way too much. That's cheating."

"Why?"

"I said one thing. You love tons of people, and each person wants their own thing. That's like using a wish to wish for infinity wishes."

"I don't love *that* many people."

"You love at least a hundred and fifty people."

"Do not." A pause. "I top out at like a hundred and ten, max."

She gave me an exasperated look, but there was fondness underneath it.

"How many people do you love?" I said.

"Two point five."

"How can you love half a person? And if you say it's Aiden Morales and it's the bottom half, I'm gonna punch you."

"Love and lust are different, I hope you know that." She looked up at the sky. "One thing. Right now. The thing you want most in the world."

"Some fries would be great."

Brit rolled her eyes. "You're no fun."

"I told you. The people-I-love thing."

4

"Yeah and I hate that you said that."

"Why?"

"Because this is a good question, not an excuse for you to be noble."

"I'm not noble."

"That's why you're noble, you don't even *know* that you're noble."

"Okay, if my answer's so shitty, then what do you want?" I said, even though I already knew what Brit wanted most in the world, right that second, and every other second too.

She didn't say it, though, just shook her head minutely. "Fries do sound good."

"You get them. I got the cones."

"I don't want to go back in there." Brit sat up. "I can't bear to watch Flora charming the shit out of everybody."

I glanced over my shoulder, where through the front window I could see Flora Feliciano standing behind the counter. Her shiny, dark brown hair was pulled back in a ponytail under her visor, her uniform shirt immaculate. She was taking a guy's order, and I watched as her eyes crinkled with a smile. The guy was definitely flirting with her, I could see it from here by the way he was leaning toward her, but I knew she couldn't tell—she rarely could. She was sweet to everyone and somehow believed that everyone was sweet back, that no one ever had ulterior motives.

She couldn't have been more different from Brit, but they were both my best friends.

I pulled a few crumpled ones out of my pocket and held them out to Brit. "She can't help it," I said. "That's just how she is."

"I know." She took the money and slid off the table. "That's why she's the point five."

She headed inside as a beat-up car pulled into the parking lot, snagging an empty spot facing the road. I recognized it—it was Heather Conlin's car. She lived just down the street from me, and I babysat her kids all the time—Cadence, who was six, and Harper, who was almost a year old.

But Heather didn't get out. Her husband, Kyle, emerged from the driver's side instead, and from the passenger's seat came a guy I had never seen before. In Acadia, that was saying something.

He looked about our age, maybe a little older—it was hard to tell. I watched as Kyle fumbled around in the back and then pulled Harper out of her car seat. Harper had what my grandma would describe as "two cents' worth of hair," which tonight was scraped together into the tiniest and cutest of pigtails, jutting off the top of her head like twin exclamation points.

Kyle hitched her up on his hip and was pulling a diaper bag out of the car when a phone began to ring.

"Ah, sorry." He tossed the bag back down and handed Harper to the guy. "Gimme one sec," he said, and then he stepped away to grab the call.

The guy stood a bit stiffly with Harper for a moment, until she pointed a chubby finger at the sky and he tilted his head back to see what had caught her eye.

"What are we looking at?"

Harper crowed something indistinguishable, and the guy nodded like it made sense.

"I see."

She babbled something else and pointed again.

"Mm. I agree."

And then she looked my way.

I did the fish face, her favorite—cheeks sucked in, flapping my hands by my head like fins. If it were just me and her in her room, I'd dance around in a circle and go "glub glub glub" to really complete the scene, but as it was, I just wiggled silently in my spot. Her face split into a smile, and she made a happy sound.

The guy grinned down at Harper, and then he followed her gaze to me.

I froze mid-flap.

Kyle sidled up beside them then, putting his phone away.

"Hey, Sophie!" he called, slinging the diaper bag over his shoulder and reaching for Harper. "Nice face!"

I lowered my hands and schooled my expression into something other than fish face as they approached. The guy's grin had faded into something neutral.

"Don't think you two have met yet," Kyle said, gesturing to the guy. "This is my brother, August. August, that's Sophie, she watches Cady and Harper."

"Nice to meet you," August said.

"That's what I've heard," I replied.

One corner of his mouth ticked up.

Kyle adjusted the strap on the diaper bag. "Still on for Tuesday night? Heather's gotta take Cady to a dance thing, so it'll just be you and this one." He smacked a kiss to Harper's cheek.

"Yup, sounds good."

"Awesome, see you then!"

They headed inside. August grabbed the door for Kyle and Harper and glanced back at me as they passed. There wasn't enough time for me to make another funny face or to smile devastatingly—not enough time to decide between the two, if I was even capable of the latter—so we just sort of looked at each other for a second.

And then he was gone.

Brit came back out clutching a brown paper bag a few minutes later. "I'm not sharing," she said, while simultaneously extending the bag toward me.

I reached in and grabbed a handful. "Did you see Kyle in there?"

"Uh-huh."

"I didn't know he had a brother."

Brit shoved a few fries in her mouth and chewed unceremoniously. "Yeah, neither did he, apparently."

"What do you mean?"

She shrugged. "Just something I heard." She wiped her hands on her shorts. "So it's Friday. What do you think? Should we go to Tropicana? *Gutter balls and matching shoes?*" She sang the last part, which was customary. It was a line from the one and only song ever written about our hometown. "Gave You My Heartland" by Megan Pleasant outlined a series of activities in Acadia day by day—Mondays at Miller's for beers, Tuesday by the lake, so on and so forth. Fridays were bowling, and although I did love the Tropicana—

"It's actually Saturday."

"Fuck, really?"

I nodded.

"Guess that's why I got fired," Brit said, and grinned, not nearly as sheepish as she should have been.

# two

**Ciara:**

You know, no one here understands the Yum Yum
  Shoppe

People are like, if your town had a McDonald's why
  didn't you just go there??

Mcflurry blah blah blah

Vanilla cone blah

I feel like you can't comprehend the Yum Yum Shoppe
  until you have experienced the Yum Yum Shoppe

Its tacky wooden decorations

The window display

Mean Kim the manager

**Sophie:**

The weird sodas

**Ciara:**

YES

Do you want Dr Pepper? You're out of luck TRY

    SOUR CREAM AND ONION SARSPARILLA

    INSTEAD

                         **Sophie:**

         Don't forget the 14 flavors of ice cream

**Ciara:**

Oh the 14 flavors

How could I?

They were so carefully curated

So hotly debated around town

                         **Sophie:**

     We have to go when you're back from school

    Dad can do that thing where he considers every

           flavor and then orders vanilla

**Ciara:**

"It's a CLASSIC, you can't DENY a CLASSIC"

WELL THEN MAYBE START BY NOT DENYING

    THE CLASSIC, DAD

MAYBE SAVE US THE DELIBERATION

                         **Sophie:**

  😆 If you could pick a 15th flavor for the list, what

                  would it be?

**Ciara:**

Something really niche

Like chewed up gum

**Sophie:**

Mothball

**Ciara:**

Old hat

**Sophie:**

Would new hat taste better than old hat?

**Ciara:**

No old hat tastes better

Like felt and history

**Sophie:**

What if the flavor wasn't a flavor at all?

What if it was a feeling?

**Ciara:**

Ooh okay. Like the feeling when you're little and you

start a brand new box of crayons

**Sophie:**

Night before Christmas excitement

**Ciara:**

Ineffable sadness

**Sophie:**

Lolololol

**Ciara:**

COME TO THE YUM YUM SHOPPE FOR

EVERYONE'S FAVORITE SEASONAL FLAVOR:

INEFFABLE SADNESS

**Sophie:**

It pairs great with old hat

"Ready?"

"Hm?" I looked up from my phone, closing out of the text thread with my sister.

Terrance Cunningham stood before me, backpack on. "I said, are you ready? For. All. Of. This." He punctuated each word with a robot move, adding a flourish at the end, and a weird hip gyration.

"I'm ready for about half of that."

"Seventy-five percent."

"Sixty-three."

"Eighty or I walk."

"We're walking anyway," I said, pushing up off the front stoop. "And you're bargaining in the wrong direction."

"Always bargain up. It's a good tactic. Throws people off."

Although school was technically over for the year, Terrance and I had one final bit of business to attend to—the last booster club meeting before the marching band's hiatus in June. We would reconvene the last week of June to practice for the July Fourth parade, and then there would be band camp, and then regular practices would resume.

Terrance and I were the future vice president and president of the Marching Pride of Acadia Student Fundraising Committee (MPASFC, which Terrance pronounced as "map as fuck" when there were no booster club members around, and we spelled out properly when there were). After this last meeting, we would be the present vice president and president proper, newly minted, and responsible in part for raising the funds necessary to send the Marching Pride of Acadia to the Tournament of Roses Parade in Pasadena this coming winter.

"No sweat," Terrance had said, back when Acadia was preparing their audition for the parade and we first joined the committee—my sophomore year, Terrance's freshman. "We only need to sell like twenty kidneys if we get picked. There are over a hundred of us. Twenty people should be willing to give up one measly kidney."

"I mean, you and I would definitely have to step up," I said. "As student leaders." I was very into being an official member of MPASFC. It would look good on my college applications, and anyway, I loved the band. I wanted to help however I could.

"You know, if we pick the most hydrated people, we could probably get better prices. Like maybe only ten kidneys, if they're super-high-quality kidneys."

"Terrance."

"Marcy Keane is always chugging those bottles of fruit water." She was, and she insisted on referring to them as *fruit infusions*, which made it insufferable. "You know she has some high-quality kidneys."

"She makes Matt drink the infusions too." Her boyfriend at the time.

"There we go. That's like forty-k worth of kidneys right there."

Kidneys didn't come up in the booster club meeting this evening. What did come up was the candy sale that just finished up (it raised about what was expected, but not as much as was hoped), and our fundraising strategies for the coming months: the Fourth of July barbecue in conjunction with the Lions Club (a quarter of all

14

proceeds from food sales would benefit the band, and the members would be responsible for cleanup), the school-wide garage sale, the formal dinner, half a dozen car washes, and, of course, the fall festival.

"So twenty percent of fall fest concession and ten percent of games will go toward fundraising," Mrs. Benson said.

Next to me, Terrance tapped his pencil absently against his notebook as Mrs. Benson talked about concession logistics. *Tap tap tap.* It started to take on a rhythm—*tap tap TAP tap, tap tap TAP tap.*

Mrs. Benson paused for a second to glance pointedly in our direction, and then resumed speaking.

Terrance looked over at me, brown eyes full of mirth, and then tapped again.

I grinned.

I had known Terrance my whole life—our moms were both teachers at Acadia Junior High. My mom taught language arts, and Terrance's mom taught science. They had been friends themselves since high school, had gone off to college together and later came back to Acadia—first my mom, then Mrs. Cunningham, who we called "Aunt Denise." A plastic-framed photo hung on our fridge showing the two of them in college, posing together wearing matching denim jackets, each with their hand on their hip. My mom had bangs teased to an impressive degree, while Aunt Denise had gorgeous box braids. *This is a genuine moment in time right here,* Aunt Denise would say when she was over, tapping the picture on the fridge. *No, this is a genuine betrayal,* my mom would reply, *seeing as you never told me how terrible I looked with that hair.* Aunt Denise would just laugh.

Mrs. Benson continued about the fall festival: "And then we've got the Megan Pleasant contest. Fifteen bucks to enter, but we'll keep ten and five will go toward the prize."

I watched Terrance print *MP contest* in his notes.

It was a tradition—every fall festival for the last eight years had featured a Megan Pleasant talent competition. It was lean the first couple of years, when she only had a few songs out. You'd end up hearing "Blue Eyes" or "Make Your Move" a dozen times or more. But now there were three albums' worth of material to work from, and you could sing any Megan song you wanted, or lip-sync (though you'd never win if you lip-synced), or dance, or do an instrumental cover. The grand prize was a cut of the entry fees, and we'd take the rest for the fundraiser.

So many people entered that it was one of the highest-earning parts of Fall Fest. There would be guaranteed at least two hours of Megan Pleasant–themed content to sit through, and the town ate that stuff up. She was by far the most famous person to come out of Acadia. In fact, she was pretty much the only famous person to come out of Acadia.

I guess Brit was a little famous in her own right—the fastest high school girls' runner in the state. They put her name up on the sign at the town line—BRIT CARTER, IHSA CLASS 1A 100M RECORD HOLDER. But that wasn't remotely like having your own fan site, or arena tour, or feature in *Rolling Stone*.

16

Terrance and I walked home together after the meeting. He toed a rock on the ground, and we kicked it back and forth as we walked.

"Party at Tegan's on Saturday," he said as we neared my house. "Should be fun."

I nodded. I was thinking about Mrs. Benson's parting words— *This won't be easy, but we just need to buckle down and focus and we can make it happen.* It was encouraging, until after a moment's contemplation she added a second *This won't be easy.*

"Obviously, I'll see you before then, but like, don't forget," Terrance said, bumping his shoulder into mine.

"You mean, don't forget to tell Flora."

I wanted Flora and Terrance to be together, with the same spirit that I would smoosh my dolls' faces together when I was little.

His lips twitched. "Don't know what you're talking about."

"Uh-huh."

"I genuinely—No idea."

"Sure," I said, heading up the steps to my front door. "Good night."

He waved and continued on down the street.

It wasn't that I had forgotten about the encounter at McDonald's on Saturday—meeting Kyle's brother for the first time. But come Tuesday night, it wasn't at the forefront of my mind as I laid Harper down in her crib.

I had spent the evening getting her fed and keeping her occupied as you did an almost-one-year-old. I put the Conlins' dog, Shepherd, out in the backyard so Harper and I could have some quality floor time. We looked at some books. We played with some toys and her favorite puppet: a black glove with a plush spider body on top (it made your fingers look like the spider legs, and it legitimately blew her mind). I got her in her jammies and sang her a made-up song about the ocean (*Harper and me, swimming in the sea, with the turtles and the dolphins and the fishy fishy fishies*). I held her and we danced around the room she shared with Cadence as I sang, turning in little circles until eventually she rested her head in the crook of my neck with a soft *thunk*.

I laid her down, switched on her night-light, peeked once more at her in the crib—her eyelids were drooping—then slipped out of the room and left the door cracked a bit.

So I didn't forget the encounter entirely, but it didn't spring to mind either that night. That's why when I swung around the corner into the kitchen and saw someone standing there, I let out an unholy yelp. I didn't register that it was August, Kyle's brother, standing in front of the open fridge and eating out of a Tupperware. All I registered was *stranger danger*.

He jerked in surprise and promptly dropped the Tupperware.

"Jesus," he said, clapping a hand to his chest.

"What are you doing?" I said, which didn't exactly make sense in the moment but came out all the same.

"I was eating." He blinked. "What are *you* doing?"

I had frozen in a weird defensive stance, which I apparently no longer needed to hold, now that the threat had been identified. "I thought you were an intruder."

"I'm not." Amusement shone in his eyes.

"Well, I know that now," I said. "You should announce yourself when you walk in somewhere."

"I didn't know anyone was home."

"You thought Harper was watching herself?"

"I mean, she does seem pretty independent for a baby. I saw her change the oil on the car yesterday."

"Yeah, but she always forgets to coat the gasket."

He grinned and then looked down to where the remains of the lasagna we had for dinner were spread across the floor.

"Sorry," he said, grin vanishing. "Sorry about that." He grabbed the roll of paper towels off the counter. I crouched down to help him clean.

"Were you eating cold lasagna?" I asked, scooping pasta remains into the Tupperware while he wiped up the trail of sauce.

"Yeah?"

"But the microwave is right there. Love yourself."

"I like it better cold."

"What?"

"Warm lasagna is too"—he waved a hand—"disorganized."

"*What?*" I repeated.

"It holds together better cold. It's more cohesive."

"Are you working on some kind of seminar about this?"

"Yup. Yeah. I am, actually. I'm the world's foremost cold-lasagna scholar."

August glanced up at me, and I couldn't explain it, but I was struck with that brand-new-box-of-crayons feeling. Every color pristine, every as-of-yet-uncolored picture a tantalizing possibility.

Acadia High School was by no means huge—there were ninety-six kids in the upcoming senior class. Over the course of my past eleven years in the Acadia school system, I had had a handful of crushes. In seventh grade, Peyton Simms and I went to the Valentine's dance together (we shared one awkward slow dance and then retreated to opposite sides of the gym). Sophomore year, Logan Turner and I hung out a few times, and kissed by the baseball field in Fairview Park (we called it quits a few days later).

That was okay. Not everyone could manage to spin out new romantic entanglements every other week like Brit did, or get together with their actual literal future spouse in high school, like Heather and Kyle. I was so busy with band, and school stuff, college applications, work. I could wait until college.

But I wasn't super opposed to the idea of *not* doing that, should the opportunity arise.

August gave the floor a final swipe and then tore off another sheet of paper towel, handing it to me. My fingers were covered in sauce from picking up pasta pieces.

"So, uh." I wiped my hands as he picked up the Tupperware and took it over to the trash can to empty it. "How long are you visiting for?"

"Not sure," he said, his back to me.

"Kind of open-ended, then?"

"Sort of." A pause. "It's just temporary."

"Like for the summer?"

Brit would inevitably make a joke about *summer lovin'*. She would be relentless. I was okay with that.

Before August could respond, there was a cry, suddenly, from Harper's room. I got to my feet. "Be right back," I said, pitching the paper towel into the trash and heading away.

He was gone when I emerged.

I checked the living room and out the back door. Shepherd bounded up, tail wagging, and I stepped aside to let him in. He followed at my heels as I opened the basement door and stuck my head downstairs, although there was nothing much down there. Just a washer and dryer by the stairs, and some old tools and piles of drywall—Kyle had been saying for ages that he was going to fix it up down there, make it into a proper room, but he hadn't quite gotten around to it yet.

The place was empty. Except for Harper and Shepherd, I was alone. August didn't return for the rest of the evening; he was still gone when Heather and Cadence returned.

"Jammy time," Heather said, ushering Cadence toward her room and then plopping her purse down on the kitchen table to riffle through it.

"August was here earlier," I said, trying to sound offhand but probably failing.

"Ah, sorry," she replied. "I forgot to give you a heads-up he might be around. Kyle said you guys ran into each other the other night, so hopefully it wasn't a total surprise." She located her wallet, thumbed through it. "I, uh, didn't want to say anything before about him coming because some stuff was still up in the air about it. But that's where Kyle was at, when he was gone last weekend. Getting August."

"Oh."

She handed me some money for the evening. "Hey, do you think you could do me a favor?"

"Sure."

I had been babysitting for the Conlins for almost three years now, ever since she and Kyle and Cadence had moved into the house two doors down from us. There were very few favors I wouldn't do for Heather.

"Maybe you could help ease him in here a little bit, introduce him to some people. Help him get settled in so when school starts he's not going in cold, not knowing anybody?"

I bit back the word *temporary* and nodded instead. "Yeah, sure."

Heather looked relieved. "Great. Thanks. That would be great."

# three

**Sophie:**

Is it hard being a new person in school?

**Ciara:**

Yes but no

I mean everyone is new at the start of college

So at the very least, you're all in the same boat

**Sophie:**

How did you make friends?

**Ciara:**

I honestly don't know

**Sophie:**

Super helpful

**Ciara:**

No, I just mean it kind of happens organically I guess

If you're lucky

There are people in your classes that you just start

    talking to

People in your dorm that you see a lot

Going to events on campus, joining clubs and stuff

                                              **Sophie:**

          You have to be good at talking to people though

**Ciara:**

Good thing I am

And you are too

                                              **Sophie:**

          You think?

**Ciara:**

Yeah

Who do you think you learned it from?

☺

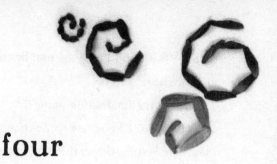

# four

I had gotten a job working at Safeway last year and had boosted my hours for the summer. I wanted to work as much as I could before band stuff started up again, so I was dedicating a fair amount of time these days to bagging groceries and collecting carts and restocking shelves.

I was helping an older lady load her grocery bags into her car, a couple of days after babysitting for Harper, when I heard voices nearby. I recognized one—it was Mrs. Benson, from the booster club. She taught at Harrison, the elementary school. Her voice carried, which was an excellent quality in a fourth-grade teacher, and also in an eavesdropping target.

Not that I was trying to eavesdrop. But I couldn't help it.

"You know, it's a huge honor, it's incredible, I get that," she was saying. "But good Lord, the money that goes into this thing, it's unfathomable."

"How's the fundraising going?"

"Honestly? I know everyone thought it was a long shot when they were getting the audition together, but I wish we had started then. With that kind of lead, we'd be all right, but as it stands . . . there's so much more to go. Michelle, you have no idea. These kids would have to sell candy bars to the moon and back."

I finished with the bags and shut the trunk. Quietly enough to not draw attention.

"Thank you, sweetie," the older lady said, and I smiled as I took her cart and steered it back toward the cart return outside the front of the store. Slow enough so I could keep listening.

"There's more to come, though," the other woman—Michelle— said. "Sponsorships, July Fourth, the sports banquet."

"Yeah, but we really need to get creative. If we do what we always do, we'll get the same we always got, which is just enough to fund those little trips here and there. Honestly, coming from Indianapolis, I just don't think she gets how chipping in two grand is impossible for most of these kids. And there's only so much money we can wring out of the people and businesses in town."

"She" was undeniably Meredith Hill, the band director, who had taken over for Mr. Haverty, the long-standing director of the Marching Pride of Acadia. He retired four years ago, and Ms. Hill had come from Indianapolis to replace him.

"I'm sure you'll figure something out," the other woman said.

Mrs. Benson nodded. "Keep your fingers crossed. I'd hate for them to have to pull out. It's happened before apparently, with other schools, but . . . I know Sam, at least, is so, so excited to go. I'm sure Becca is too."

"Oh yeah."

"Well, keep it between us, and I'll keep you posted."

"Sounds good. Night, Jen."

"Night."

I slotted the cart into the one in front of it and headed inside.

I volunteered at the library on Saturday mornings.

It wasn't a huge place—just one room, with the checkout desk in the middle. The general-fiction shelves sat to the right in tall rows, with the nonfiction shelves lining the room. The kids and teen books were tucked on the other side, in each of the corners.

The head librarian was named Mel. She was probably mid-fifties, and humorless, but she knew everything there was to know about books. I'd swear there wasn't a book in there she hadn't read.

*She knows everything*, Flora said. *She's like the internet.*

She was possibly better than the internet sometimes. I'd volunteered there since freshman year, and Mel had never once redirected to an ad for male enhancement.

When I got to work this morning, I took a seat in the Kids Korner.

*Why do we have to spell it like that? Why can't we just spell "corner" the normal way?* I had asked, when Mel first announced her plan to redesign the children's area.

*It's for kids*, Mel had answered simply.

*Yeah, even more reason we should spell it right, don't you think?*

She looked at me, deadpan: *It's cute.*

So every few months I hand-lettered a new seasonal banner with KIDS KORNER outlined on it in sparkle paint, and it was cute, I guess—if an inconsistent foundation in spelling could be considered cute.

The Kids Korner faced the teen area in the opposite corner, which had its own banner, although it didn't change to match the seasons. It was a permanent fixture, a large purple sign with cutout bubble letters attached to it spelling out the words TEEN ZONE.

The Teen Zone sign had appeared after I started volunteering there. Mel never discussed it, but it was a source of great delight among my friends—so much so that we christened the Cunninghams' pole shed, where we did the majority of our hanging out, Teen Zone 2.

*After all, it's where the teens are at*, Brit had said. *It's the zone for teens. We almost can't exist in any other kind of zone. Child Zone? Forget it. Adult Zone? Fuck that noise. I am for the Teen Zone only.*

She also often used it as a euphemism: *I want to put my Teen Zone on his Teen Zone. I want her all up in my Teen Zone.*

Today I sat across from the non-euphemistic, original Teen Zone with my copy of *The College Collective*. The library was pretty empty for a Saturday morning—a couple of people wandering the fiction shelves, one tween girl thumbing through a stack of novels in the Teen Zone. But there were no kids to populate Kids Korner, so I flipped open my book.

The College Collective was a website whose college application timeline I had adopted. Unlike some of the other sites that guided more broadly, they broke it down month by month for your last two years of high school. Things to consider, action steps you should take, tips and helpful suggestions. I sent away for their hard copy handbook at the beginning of sophomore year and received a thick spiral-bound book with a multicultural band of smiling kids on the front, arms slung around one another. It was well-worn now, I had thumbed through it so often.

I had been one full year under the College Collective's guidance (it started with SOPHOMORE YEAR, JUNE), and, accordingly, I felt like I was in good shape. I had taken the SAT and ACT early, with plenty of time to retake (I knew I could do better on math). I had created my general list of schools, and I was prepared to narrow them down this summer to a finalized list that I would begin targeting closely. I had focused on my grades this past year (junior year transcript is essential), and my extracurriculars (homecoming committee, band). I volunteered (the library), and I had a leadership position (MPASFC), and work experience (the grocery store).

Today I was staring at the chapter labeled JUNIOR YEAR, JUNE–AUGUST: THE EVE OF SENIOR YEAR, but my mind kept wandering. I couldn't help but glance toward the bulletin board tacked up between a set of shelves in the Teen Zone. Right in the center was a clipping from the front page of the *Acadia News*, an old edition that had been pinned up for some time. MARCHING PRIDE OF ACADIA SELECTED FOR TOURNAMENT OF ROSES PARADE.

No part of the *College Collective* handbook covered how to raise the money for something like that. It had tips for financial aid and scholarship opportunities, and although I definitely needed both of those things for college to be a remote possibility, the money I needed right now was for a different purpose.

It was a huge honor—bigger even than marching in the Macy's Thanksgiving Day Parade, which Acadia did in 2007. We were a small high school, but it's not like there was much else to do but sports or marching anyway, and everyone pretty much participated in one or the other or both. Sure, there was other stuff—Flora did art club, Terrance was in the school play last year—but the band and the football team ranked first and second in order of importance. (Although the football team probably saw it as the other way around.)

I thought about what I overheard Mrs. Benson saying in the parking lot the other day. *These kids would have to sell candy bars to the moon and back.*

I hadn't really thought about the possibility of not raising the money. The booster club would pull through. They always did.

But maybe she was right to be worried. Nothing we'd done had ever cost as much before, and if we did all the same things we always did . . . maybe we wouldn't make it.

My thoughts were interrupted by the pound of little-kid feet, and when I looked up, Cadence had appeared, dragging August behind her. I waved when he caught my eye.

"Sophie, what should we read that's good?" Cadence said.

"They're all good."

"*Especially* good."

I smiled, setting aside the *College Collective* handbook (would Mel endorse spelling it *Kollege Kollective*, or was it no longer cute when higher education was concerned?) and getting to my feet. As I helped Cadence pick out a few books, I heard a baby-pitched squeal from near the front desk and saw Heather going after Harper, who hadn't quite mastered her center of gravity yet, having only just begun to take on walking. Heather scooped her up and waved when she saw me. She gestured over to the general-fiction shelves and then retreated with Harper in her arms.

"Let's read, Uncle August," Cadence said after she had made her selections, tugging on August's arm until he sank into a nearby yellow beanbag chair. She shoved a book in his hands and squashed in next to him.

They read, and I flipped back open to JUNIOR YEAR, JUNE–AUGUST. But really I was listening in on the random voices August was giving the characters, after Cadence complained that there wasn't enough variation between them.

"The elephant can't sound the same as the pig. They should sound different."

August gave the pig a super deep voice, and the elephant an indeterminable accent.

They had read through a few by the time Heather came over.

"Okay, let's pick out the ones we want to take home," she said, gesturing Cadence up and following her back to one of the low shelves crammed with picture books.

August watched them for a moment from the beanbag chair, and then stood, stretched, and moved to look at a shelf nearer to me.

"So where was the elephant supposed to be from?" I said, because I was pretty sure he wasn't interested in browsing picture books.

"Scotland," he said, like it was obvious, and when I raised an eyebrow, "Scotland adjacent?"

I smiled, first at him and then down at the kids on the *College Collective* cover. I knew their names from the photo caption inside— *Jeff, Jackie, Sonja, Han, and Fadia enjoy time out on the quad.* I liked to imagine that Jeff and Jackie had dated briefly, but she left him for Sonja. The smile she and Sonja were sharing was just too knowing.

This didn't seem like a solid avenue of conversation with August. At least not yet.

(I had mentioned it to Brit once, and she took one look and said, *Oh yeah, Jackie and Sonja have totally boned down.*)

"You disappeared the other night," I said after a pause. "You should've left a note."

"Why?"

"So I would know if you were really gone or not. I thought you might have been waiting to jump out at me."

"Why would I do that?"

"Because it's funny. Well, it's not funny if you're the person being jumped at, but it's funny if you're the person doing the jumping."

"You speak from experience?"

"I used to pull that shit on my sister all the time when we were kids. Hiding in closets, or under the bed so I could reach out for her foot, like in a horror movie."

"I've never done that."

"You don't know what you're missing," I said. "Anyway, if you'd left a note, I would've known when you were coming back." He was looking at me strangely. "Not that I was, like. Anticipating. Your return." I swallowed. "It's just polite."

He nodded. "Next time, I'll leave a note."

"Good." I liked the idea of there being a next time.

His lips twitched, eyes shining. "'Dear Sophie, mind your own business. Fondest wishes, August.'"

"Rude."

"I said 'fondest wishes.'"

I fought a smile.

I thought of Heather's words the other night—*Maybe you could help ease him in here a little bit, introduce him to some people?*

"So," I said. "This girl from school, Tegan Wendall? She's having this thing tonight and a bunch of people are going, so, uh, if you wanted to come . . . you know. You could."

"You're asking me to a party?"

"Yeah." But that felt too much like a declaration. "I mean, no. But yes. I'm inviting you, but it's not like, *with me*, it's just . . . if you want to meet new people or whatever."

For a moment I'd swear August's face said yes, but then his mouth said: "I probably shouldn't. But thanks."

My mouth replied: "Cool, yeah, maybe next time," but I'm not exactly sure how my face responded. August wouldn't know either, though, because he had already turned toward Cadence, who had returned with a large stack of books in her arms. Heather had corralled Harper and was heading toward the checkout desk.

"See you around, Soph!" Heather called over one shoulder, as Cadence beamed up at August.

"I got more to take home!" she said.

August reached for them.

"I can do it!" She turned away quickly, tightening her arms around the books.

"You're right, that's way too big a stack for me anyway," he said to Cadence, and then to me: "See you later."

"Fondest wishes!" I called.

He grinned, quick and bright, and then they were heading away.

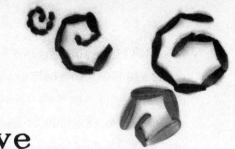

# five

"Those shoes are stupid," Brit said, gesturing to Flora's high-heeled sandals. "You're gonna regret it."

"I will not. I look cute."

"We're literally biking there. At least wear sneakers to ride."

"I'm gonna sit on Sophie's handlebars."

"You know Sophie has terrible balance and you're gonna end up on my handlebars, and I'm not letting you on my handlebars when you can obviously bike yourself with the right fricking shoes on. Sophie tell her—Where are you going?"

I was already crossing the lawn. "To Heather's."

"Why? She won't drive us."

"To see if August wants to come."

"I thought he told you no."

Technically, it was an *I probably shouldn't.* I didn't know how to parse that exactly, but I figured it was worth one more shot, just in case. I told Heather I would introduce him to people. This was due diligence.

"Just gimme a minute," I said, cutting across the neighboring yard to the Conlins' house.

Brit huffed and set her bike down to follow. Flora carefully picked her way after us, in her platform sandals and short shorts—the kind that were *more ass than short*, according to Brit.

"This is Kyle's secret brother?" Flora asked.

"He's not a *secret brother*," I hissed.

"When you have a brother no one knows about, that's a secret brother," Brit said.

I could see the TV on through the front window. I stepped up to the door and knocked.

"No one say 'secret brother.'"

Shepherd barked from inside, followed by the sound of some shuffling.

"Clandestine sibling," Brit whispered, before the door swung open.

"Hey, girls." Heather had Harper in her arms, who was squirming to get away from her.

"Hey. We're going to Tegan's, and I was wondering if August wanted to come."

Heather's face lit up. "Yes! He does!"

"Really? 'Cause he told Sophie he didn't." Brit wasn't much for second chances.

"He'll be right out."

August shuffled out a few moments later.

"Have fun! Back by curfew!" Heather called, and shut the door definitively.

We all stood for a moment. It wasn't uncomfortable per se. But it wasn't super comfortable either.

"This is Brit and Flora," I said to August, and "This is August," to them.

"Nice to meet you," Flora said.

"That's what I've heard," he replied, and my eyes snapped toward him.

"That was my joke! I said that when we met!"

"Did you?" His face was totally stoic, but there was something alight in his eyes.

"I did."

"Oh. So you own the copyright?"

"Yes. That shit is in the Library of Congress."

He smiled, and it was a moment before I realized that Flora and Brit were both staring at us.

"Uh, so—"

"You got a bike?" Brit said.

"No." August looked back at the house. "Maybe Kyle—"

"You can borrow mine!" Flora exclaimed. "I'll ride on the handlebars."

Tegan Wendall's house was just a little ways outside of town, off 49. It was nice—surrounded by trees, set back a bit with a big yard.

We left our bikes propped against the garage and walked toward the back, where there was a fire pit with some plastic lawn chairs arranged around it. A crowd had already formed.

It was almost entirely people from band—Tegan was on the color guard—and I knew basically everyone, but we immediately zeroed in on one person in particular.

Dashiell Cunningham was standing a little apart from the groups that had formed, clutching a plastic cup. To most, he would appear disinterested in his surroundings, but I could see the tightness around his mouth, which eased immediately when Brit ran up and pushed him playfully with both hands.

He barely jostled. He was the size of a small mountain.

*Dash got all the height and Terrance got everything else*, I had heard someone say of the Cunningham brothers once. Brit had shut that down with a simple but pointed *Excuse me?* and as such, I had never heard it again.

Dash, Brit, and I had been in class together since preschool. I remember him bringing a plastic dump truck into show-and-tell back then, holding it under one arm and looking out at the class with solemn eyes while the teacher gently urged him to tell us more about it.

"It's a truck," he had said.

"What kind of truck?"

"A good truck."

That was Dash. *The most serious four-year-old I've ever met*, my mom would say. *Always looked like he was trying to solve the world's problems.*

She and Aunt Denise would trade off watching us sometimes, when the other had to stay late at work. *But when Dash smiled,* Mom would always add, *it was like the sun coming out from behind the clouds.*

Tonight Dash nodded at August when I introduced him.

"Where's Terrance?" Brit said.

"Getting drinks," Dash replied.

"Good idea." Brit turned to us. "Dash is covered. We need boring sodas for Sophie and Flora." She pointed at August. "What about you?"

"Surprise me," he said.

I followed Brit into the house, because a surprise-me drink from her could be lethal.

"So what's going on with you and the secret brother?" she asked when we reached the kitchen. She started uncapping a two-liter as I set out some cups.

"Nothing," I said.

She eyed me for a moment. "But you want there to be." She raised and lowered her eyebrows several times as she began pouring drinks. "You want to get your Teen Zone on his Teen Zone."

*"Brit."*

"Tell me I'm wrong."

"You're not right."

"That's a certified Sophie lie right there," she said, and forced two cups of soda into my hand. "Take that to your boyfriend. Tell him you're the surprise."

"I hate you."

"Now that's a certified Brit *I love you*," she replied, which was entirely accurate.

At any party or school thing, we always managed to carve out our own little spot. This time, it was at a wooden picnic table back by the trees, a little ways from the fire pit. Close enough that there was still light, but not so close that it was too hot. One of the drum majors, Jason Sosa, was nearby, strumming on an acoustic guitar, while two girls from the woodwinds—Alexa Valenti and Jessica Walsh—watched lovingly. Brit rolled her eyes at me in a *Get a load of them* kind of way, and I acted like I didn't remember that she had a momentary crush on Jason Sosa in the seventh grade, and one on Alexa Valenti in eighth.

Terrance and I told everyone about the booster club meeting, which Brit pretended to find really boring. I had had to convince her—hard—to even march this year.

"It's a huge commitment," she had said, sitting on the wall out by the athletic fields, playing slapjack with Dash. "I hate commitment. Anyway, you know I need to train." She had been spending more and more time at the track or in the gym, conditioning. She was trying to shave time off her 200 meter.

"Training sounds like a commitment," I said.

She made a face.

"You're a good drummer. We need you."

"One more drum's not gonna make a difference."

"Brit." I blinked. "Please."

She had stared back for a long moment and then rolled her eyes. "Jesus. Okay. Fine."

"You gotta teach me how you did that," Dash said with a grin.

Tonight, we seemed to be the only people talking band-related stuff, if the snatches of conversation from the surrounding groups were any indication. Jason Sosa probably wasn't thinking about fundraising during yet another flaccid acoustic ballad.

"The July Fourth barbecue should be good," I said, when we reached the end of our rundown. "But we need to be able to bring in some real money at Fall Fest."

Terrance took a sip of his drink and looked at me innocently. "Is this the year you guys finally win the Megan Pleasant contest?"

"That was *one time*," Brit said. "In sixth grade. Let it go."

"I'll never forget those moves," Terrance replied. "Brit looked like one of those inflatable guys at a car dealership. Sophie looked like a knife caught in a garbage disposal."

"What did I look like?" Flora asked.

"Perfect, right?" Dash supplied.

"The best dancer ever seen by human eyes," Brit guessed, before Terrance could answer.

"Who's Megan Pleasant?" August said from next to me.

Terrance, probably about to expound on Flora's talents as a dancer, froze. "Who is Megan—*Who?* Who is Megan Pleasant?" he repeated, expression aghast. He turned to me. "Who is this kid? Where did you find him?"

"She's a singer," I told August. "From Acadia. She's pretty famous."

"Never heard of her."

"'Gave You My Heartland'? 'Letters Home'?"

"Sorry."

"She was on TV," Flora said helpfully. "They play her stuff on the radio."

"What kind of music?"

"Country."

He grimaced. "Oh."

"It's not terrible."

"I've never heard a country song that doesn't suck."

"Maybe you haven't listened to the right ones," I said.

"I know a country song that doesn't suck," Brit interjected. "Written by a small-town boy with big-city dreams—"

Terrance's eyes grew wide. "Everybody needs to shut up right now right this second."

A slow smile spread across Dash's face. "Brit, does it take place on a farm?"

"It sure does, Dashiell," Brit said. "Inexplicably."

"Does it involve . . . footwear?"

"Oh yes."

"Sneakers?"

"Nope."

"Flip-flops?"

"No."

Terrance stood up. "I'm leaving."

"Clogs," Dash said sagely.

"Not clogs, dear friend."

"This is the last time you'll ever see me," Terrance said, and started away.

"Terrance wrote a country song when we were in middle school," I told August.

"'The Girl with the Brown Boots,'" Brit said with relish, and Terrance doubled back instantly.

"It was 'The Girl with the Blue Boots' and you know it. Her eyes were brown, her boots were blue, that's the first damn line of the song, Brit."

"'The girl with the blue boooooooots,'" Brit half yelled, half sang.

"I was ahead of my time!" Terrance said loudly, and then to August, at a lower decibel: "Man, I was ahead of my time, okay? A few years later, everybody starts doing the whole retro-throwback thing, and I was right there on the cusp of it. Just without the *proper respect*—"

"It's great because there are so many rhymes for the word 'boots,'" Brit said.

"—that a *true visionary* deserves—"

"Shoots," I said, just as Flora said, "Roots."

Dash: "Toots."

Brit: "Flutes."

"Cahoots?" August offered.

"Nah, that's too good," Dash said.

With that, Terrance turned and really left. I was worried that he was actually mad, until he returned with the acoustic guitar that Jason Sosa had earlier. A quick glance around the backyard revealed that Jason and Alexa were now making out fervently by the shed.

Terrance planted himself on top of the picnic table, the guitar over one knee. "Fine. Let's do this," and he began to strum, and to sing—poorly, but with conviction—"'Her eyes were brown, her boots were blue—'"

"Wait wait wait!" August held up a hand. "Can we guess the next line?"

Brit snorted. "You say that like you think the lyrics to 'The Girl with the Blue Boots' aren't indelibly burned into our brains for all eternity."

"You all know this song?"

"We're literally going to meet Jesus with the words to this song still in our heads," Dash said.

"That being said," Brit added, "I'll pay you a thousand dollars if you get it right."

Brit had probably seventeen dollars to her name. She went through money like it was water. But it was also a pretty safe bet.

August thought for a long moment, and then: "'She had blond hair . . . and blue shoes'?"

Terrance looked offended. "That doesn't even scan. And why would I mention the shoes twice in a row?"

"Like the real lyric is so much better," I said.

"Hey!" he squawked.

"Okay, what is it?" August asked.

Terrance began again: "'Her eyes were brown, her boots were blue. The cat meowed, the cow said moo—'"

"Wait, what?" August said. *"What?"*

"He had to set the scene," Brit explained. "You see, the animal sounds establish the fact that we're on a *farm*—"

"I was a visionary!" Terrance bellowed. "UNDERMINED IN MY PRIME!"

"Oh man." August put a hand over his mouth, but the crinkles at the corners of his eyes gave away his smile.

"You have to hear the whole thing. The lyrics don't make sense out of context," Terrance insisted.

"Be careful, though," I said, leaning toward August a little. "If you listen to the song all the way through, you die in seven days."

"It's true," Dash said. "We're all dead right now."

August grinned full-out now.

The song didn't get better from there. The bridge—the height of "rhymes with boots"—was especially something.

Terrance finished with a flourish and looked at August, eyebrows raised expectantly. "What do you think?"

August looked conflicted—half like he was seriously considering it, half like he wanted to burst out laughing. Finally he spoke: "I mean. It's so bad it's almost good again."

Terrance paused. "I'll take it!" And then yelled, "ONE MORE TIME!"

We let out a cheer.

# six

A couple of hours later, we were attempting to cajole Brit into Dash's car.

We had sung, we had danced, and she had drunk. I was familiar with the stages of Brit drunkenness—there was the saying-things-she-wouldn't-normally-say stage, the hands-on-both-my-shoulders stage, the grinding-up-on-Aiden-Morales stage, arms in the air, liquid sloshing over the rim of her cup.

It had taken some doing to get her away, and now she had one arm slung around my neck, the other around August's, still clutching an empty plastic cup in one hand as we made our way through the house, toward the front door. Dash was bringing his car around.

Brit could walk on her own, but she leaned heavily on us

anyway, swaying toward me. "Do you think Cassie knows her skirt is ugly?"

"She does now," August said.

She snorted and then leaned toward him. "Question."

"Yeah?"

"Who even are you anyway?"

His lips twitched. "August Shaw, so I'm told."

"Different last name," she said.

"Hm?"

"Conlin. Shaw."

His expression didn't change, but his lips pressed together slightly as he reached for the front door.

"You're not bad-looking, you know," Brit continued.

"Geez, Brit, come on," I said.

"He's not! It's a compliment! *You're just her type*," she told August in a loud whisper, jerking her head toward me. I squeezed her wrist where it hung down around my neck, praying she wouldn't mention Teen Zones. "And I go in for that whole kinda vibe sometimes myself, if I'm being honest." She held up one finger. "Sometimes. Don't get any ideas."

Now August looked amused. "I have no ideas. I've never had an idea in my life."

It was my turn to snort.

We waited for Dash out front. Inside, they cranked "Gave You My Heartland," which means people had reached peak intoxication. A sing-along began after the opening chords.

"Hey, this is her." Brit batted at August's arm. "Good ol' Megan Pleasant. Meggy P. Pride of Acadia right there." I mentally cataloged *Meggy P.* for future use. I didn't usually use drunk-Brit things against normal Brit. But Meggy P. was too good.

I watched as Brit spun around, started dancing, and then stopped suddenly, swaying a little on the spot. "You know who should sing at the Megan Pleasant contest?" She smiled, broad and pure. "Megan Pleasant."

Then she belched.

"Except she would probably win," she continued, "and then Chelsea Peters would cry 'cause she's been trying to win that shit for the last hundred years." She tossed her cup aside. "No one wants her crappy indie version of 'Steel Highway.'" She pointed to August. "When you sing 'Steel Highway,' you have to put the motherfucking steel on that motherfucking highway. None of that . . . warbling shit. Fucking . . . ukulele. If Megan Pleasant heard that, she would slap Chelsea. In the *face.*"

"Where else would she slap her?" August murmured.

"On the ass?" I said.

"Like a *Go team!* kind of thing?"

I nodded. "Maybe if she was into it."

Headlights appeared, cutting through the circle drive in front of Tegan's house, and Dash's pride and joy, his 1992 Cutlass Supreme, pulled up in front of us.

He had bought it from an old lady down the street with the money he made last summer, and fixed it up as best he could. I remember when he first showed it off to us. *It's an antique*, he had said, because a car had to be twenty-five years old to be one, and the Cutlass just qualified. There had to be a pretty deep valley of coolness stretching between a barely antique car and a definitely antique car, but no one pointed that out, because Dash was well and truly thrilled. He had smiled that *sun coming out from behind the clouds* smile—an impossibly wide one where you could see his top and bottom teeth, pure joy, like a little kid.

I opened the door and ushered Brit in.

"What about my bike?" she said as I got her seat belt fastened.

"August will ride it. Flora can ride her own."

A worried crease appeared on her forehead. "What about her shoes? She can't pedal in those shoes."

"She'll be all right."

"Here." She fumbled against the seat belt, reaching down and pulling off one of her sneakers. "Take my shoes."

"Brit—"

"Give Flora my shoes." She wrangled the other one off and forced them both on me. I took them, battered and warm.

"Drive safe, okay?"

Dash nodded, and I stepped back, shutting the door.

The window was down, and Brit waved to me like we might never see each other again.

"I love you, Sophie."

"Love you too."

"Give Flora my shoes."

"I will."

They drove off, brake lights disappearing in the distance.

It was quiet.

"I was thinking of heading out too," August said after a moment. "Should I give you my shoes? Is that like a parting thing here?"

"Yeah. Get drunk, comment on people's appearances, talk about country music. Give away your shoes."

"Noted."

"You should take Brit's bike. Flora's was probably a bit small for you." My eyes raked his frame for a moment, and then I tried to pretend like they hadn't. "You can just leave it outside my house."

His brow furrowed. "But someone might steal it."

"Who?"

"I don't know. Like. Vagrants or something."

"This is Acadia. Most people don't lock their front doors."

"Most people are pretty deluded."

"Ooh, edgy," I said, starting around the side of the house toward the garage, where our bikes were stowed. August followed. "Are you gonna school me all about life in the big mean city?"

"Saint Louis is not the big mean city, good Lord. It's just . . . a city."

"You're from Saint Louis?"

"Yeah."

"Huh."

"What?"

"I don't know. I guess I pictured you from . . . a bigger, meaner city." Not that Saint Louis wasn't big—just that I had been there before. I had imagined August from somewhere . . . less familiar, I guess.

"Which city is the big mean city? Chicago?"

"No. Maybe. Just like. A big place. Lots of people. Anonymity. Graffiti. Cool shoes and stuff."

"Like those?" He pointed to Brit's beat-up sneakers.

"These were cool once upon a time. She just keeps running through them." They were all worn down in the heels, the rubber starting to come apart. Brit did everything hard—when she was into something, it was all in, whether it was partying or friendship or track. Especially track.

"She's the fastest runner in the state, you know," I said, fumbling with one of the rubber flaps on the soles.

"Really?"

"Mm-hm. In the hundred meter. She had the two-hundred record too, but this girl from Collinsville beat her by a third of a second at their last invitational." I made a face. "Fastest runner for girls, I should say. But she'd hate if you made that distinction. She wants to be fastest, period. Go to the Olympics and all that. She takes it really seriously."

I didn't know why I was telling him all this. I hadn't drunk anything—I didn't need to, apparently, to say what I was really thinking. Sometimes I wondered if Brit played it up as an excuse to say anything she thought out loud.

Then again, maybe if I had been drinking, I would've had the courage to ask August out on a date. Because I had pretty much decided—I liked him. I didn't know him very well, but that was what dating was for, right? And anyway, there were so few people in town that when someone came along that you were actually interested in, you had to go ahead and do something about it.

But it was easier to talk about Brit, so I just fumbled with the laces on her sneakers and said, "She'll definitely get a track scholarship somewhere."

August nodded, and I wondered if he was bored. His expression gave no indication either way, decidedly neutral.

"It's like her . . . thing," I added, like that somehow conveyed the importance. It was less complicated-sounding than "revenge quest."

He nodded again as we reached the garage, and then asked, "What's your thing?"

*You could be my thing. Your thing could be my*—God, that was . . .

"Band," I said, "I guess." Even though there was no guessing about it.

"Kind of got that from earlier. What's map as fuck?"

"MPASFC, the student fundraising committee. I'm the president. Well, the new president. Kayla Jenkins was president until last week. She's going to nursing school—she graduated—so I like, ascended or whatever."

"Very biblical."

I smiled. "What about you?"

"Thing-wise?"

"Yeah."

"I don't know. Nothing serious. Not like, Olympics serious, at least. I played in jazz band in middle school, but I was pretty terrible."

"Really?" If August was going to stay in Acadia, he could join band. He could march with us. "What'd you play?"

"Saxophone."

"Of course you did."

His lips quirked. "What's that mean?"

"I don't know. It just . . . fits."

"What do you play?"

"I'm the world's most average clarinet player," I said, and then it was quiet.

Had we used up all our conversation? It wasn't ideal. I'd have to think of topics of discussion if we were going to go out—questions to ask and stuff like that.

But it was late, and maybe we were both tired, and also maybe it wasn't so bad being able to be quiet with someone.

"I should probably get going," he said finally, and I probably should've asked then, in the silence, but the opportunity had dissolved. "Will you . . . I mean, will you get home safe? I could hang around. . . ."

"Nah, I'll wait for Flora and Terrance." Terrance was busy serenading people—which made me wonder if it's not so much the skill that really matters but the confidence—and Flora was with him.

We had never collectively acknowledged it as a group, but Flora was undeniably the Girl with the Blue Boots. She "passed the time by playing flute," and she had a pair of blue fake leather lace-up boots that she wore all the time when we were in middle school. And Terrance did love her "like the stars in the sky, yeah, like a lovestruck guy." I guess the farm thing was a misdirect.

I waved a hand at the bikes. "Brit's is the green one."

"Thanks."

"Now I just need your shoes, and then you can be on your way."

It was August's turn to smile.

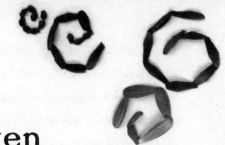

# seven

I replayed the party in my mind that night as I got ready for bed. Put on my pajamas, switched off the light, and stared at the ceiling, thinking about Terrance singing, Brit swaying back and forth with one arm slung around Dash's shoulders, Flora's bright eyes as we all sang along. I thought about August, gently bopping his head, looking like he might join in on the chorus, though he never did.

And then, somehow, amid everything, Brit's words sprang into my mind:

*You know who should sing in the Megan Pleasant contest? Megan Pleasant.*

Ten years ago, Megan was a contestant on *America's Next Country Star*.

At seven, I was more of a fan of the boy bands of the moment and Disney Channel tweens with fledgling singing careers. But the whole town watched *America's Next Country Star*. The live shows were broadcast in the high school, projected in the auditorium so we could all watch fifteen-year-old Megan clutching the microphone, bowing her head and praying before singing "This Kiss" for Nineties Week, or "Jolene" for Classics Week, or "Our Song" for My Idol Week. We all watched Megan get further and further along in the competition, and before the semifinals, they even sent a camera crew to Acadia to get footage of people holding signs saying things like WE LOVE MEGAN and ACADIA'S PROUD OF YOU.

She was the youngest contestant on the show, and she became an absolute fan favorite. People printed up T-shirts with OH MY STARS on them, because that was her constant exclamation—when she got through to the live shows, when a Grammy winner showed up to mentor her. I liked "oh my stars," but my favorite was when she would try something that didn't work (a particular run, a song that maybe didn't quite suit), she'd shrug and smile and say, "Worth a shot." (There were "Worth a shot" shot glasses sold at Miller's for ages, which some parents deemed inappropriate, but they sold nonetheless.)

Megan made it to the finals but didn't win. She came in third place, but it wasn't long before she had gotten a recording contract anyway, and soon there was a first single, a first video, a first album. Soon she was Megan Pleasant, country singer, instead of Megan Pleasant, reality-show hopeful. Either way, she remained Megan Pleasant, Acadia's hometown girl.

Pine Valley Library

07/22/2019 6:28:56 PM          910-798-6390

Automated Telephone Renewals 910-798-6320

Renew Online at http://www.nhclibrary.org

Title:          Hungry hearts :
Item ID:        34200014479279
**Due:          08/12/2019**

Title:          Technically, you started it /
Author:         Johnson, Lana Wood
Item ID:        34200014480640
**Due:          08/12/2019**

Title:          Famous in a small town /
Author:         Mills, Emma, 1989-
Item ID:        34200013227356
**Due:          08/12/2019**

**Fine Balance for      $0.00
This Account**

| Title: | Hungry hearts / |
| Item ID: | 34200014473279 |
| Due: | 08/12/2019 |

| Title: | Technically, you started it / |
| Author | Johnson, Lana Wood |
| Item ID: | 34200014480540 |
| Due: | 08/12/2019 |

| Title: | Famous in a small town / |
| Author | Mills, Emma, 1989- |
| Item ID: | 34200013272356 |
| Due: | 08/12/2019 |

Fine Balance for    $0.00
This Account

Realistically I had probably seen her around town, before she became famous. But the first time I remember seeing her—really seeing her—she was seventeen and was set to perform for Acadia's Fourth of July celebration. She was two years off of *America's Next Country Star*, and her first album was out. "Gave You My Heartland" had just gone certified gold.

I was in fourth grade, and we had to write essays about our heroes. I was one of the winners picked for my grade. The prize was to meet Megan.

She gave us T-shirts with "Megan's Champions" on them. It was a community-outreach program she was doing—Megan's Champions would get together to rake leaves or carry groceries for old people or whatever. Like a renegade Girl Scouts or something, and they would post videos about it online, encouraging people to do the same in their towns.

I became an official Megan's Champion that day. And I fell a little bit in love with Megan too.

I didn't know how to describe it at the time, but she was the most beautiful person I'd ever seen. She had the prettiest nails— painted pale pink—and long shiny brown hair, olive-toned skin. I had never seen anyone cooler in real life, I had never even imagined anyone as cool as she was, not even Ciara, who was infinitely cooler than me. It was a little like when you play Barbies, and you pick yours, your girl, and you say stuff about her accordingly—*My girl does this; my girl does that.* I wanted to be Megan Pleasant, but I also wanted her to be My Girl.

She took a picture with all of us, in our Megan shirts, and I got to stand right next to her. I kept this picture up in a place of honor in my room for years after, and even now, it was pinned to my bulletin board, only partially obscured by pictures of me and Flora and Brit at homecoming, of Dash and Terrance posed in front of the Cutlass.

Tonight I slipped out of bed and went into the living room, where my dad's old computer was set up on a desk shoved in the corner by the pass-through to the kitchen. It was slow as hell to start up, but I wanted to type this out for real, so I waited, and while I did, I composed the message in my head.

When it finally booted up, I went to a site I visited often when I was a kid. It wasn't the official Megan Pleasant website—that had changed drastically over the years—but a site that had remained relatively unchanged since that meeting back in fourth grade. The official Megan's Champions page.

That picture from July Fourth was still posted. I was the smallish one to Megan's right, grinning widely in my bright blue shirt.

There was still a tab to the left of the screen—MEGAN WANTS TO HEAR FROM YOU!

I'd sent Megan messages often when I was a kid. It was like having a pen pal who didn't write me back, but I wrote all the same. I hadn't sent anything in years, but it still seemed, somehow, like a more direct line to her. Maybe no one checked these messages—maybe they never had, maybe they were just sent into the vacuum of the internet—but she didn't even have an email form on her official site, just a place where you could sign up for her mailing list ("EXCLUSIVE content! TOUR and TICKET info! SPECIAL NEWS from Megan to YOU!").

The Megan's Champions site had no such sign-up. Just the same old tab, the same old form. I clicked on MEGAN WANTS TO HEAR FROM YOU!, and it popped up.

I took a breath, paused with my hands over the keys.

*Dear Megan,*

*I am a junior (well now a senior I guess!) at Acadia High School in Illinois (Did you know there is an Acadia High School in California too?). I am writing because the Marching Pride of Acadia is going to march in the Rose Parade this coming year. That is, if we can afford it! I'm not trying to ask for money, but I am writing to ask you if you would possibly be willing to play a concert, or at least sing a song or two, at the fall festival in Acadia this year. We will be having the annual Megan Pleasant contest, and we would also be honored if you would be willing to act as a judge. We believe you could drastically help our fundraising efforts and would be so, so grateful if you were able to come. I know you must have a super busy schedule, but I really appreciate your consideration.*

*Thank you so much!*
*Sophie Kemper*

It had been a long time since Megan had been back to Acadia. Maybe it was possible. Maybe she would come and play the fall festival.

I left my contact info at the bottom and pressed send.

It was worth a shot.

# eight

A giant sign stood along I-70 on the way to Acadia that read, in imposing block letters, two feet tall each, WHERE WILL YOU SPEND ETERNITY?

The follow-up sign came a tenth of a mile or so later, equally imposing, white letters on a black background: JESUS CHRIST HAS THE ANSWER.

We had a group chat, the five of us, called WHERE WILL YOU SPEND ETERNITY, and since its inception, everyone had to periodically sound off with our own answer to the question. Like someone would ask WWYSE, and Brit would say, *At the YYS watching Tyler chew his fucking nails,* or Terrance would say, *In line at the Burger Shack because you know those onion rings take time,* or Dash would say, *Praying for y'all. Seriously.*

Flora always gave a very sweet and well-meaning answer to

the actual question, like *w/ my best friends in the world!!!!!* or *w/ our Lord praising Him!!!!!!* 🙌🙌🙌🙌🙌 ☺☺☺☺☺☺☺ ♡♡♡.

The morning after Tegan's party, I tapped out a message to WWYSE:

*What if Megan Pleasant played the fall festival?*

No one answered immediately. Not that I thought they would, but part of me had hoped it would instantly spark a conversation. *Great idea, Sophie! That'll totally raise the money we need! She'll definitely do it!*

So I went on:

*Like what if she gave a concert?*

*People would flip their shit*

*She hasn't been here in a few years, and she's pretty famous now*

*We could raise a lot of $$$ for the parade*

Brit replied a little while later. I was surprised she was awake.

*I see a couple problems with that*

*Such as?* I replied.

*For starters, she hasn't been here in a few years, and she's pretty famous now*

*So?*

*So. . . . . . . how exactly are you going to convince her to come?*

The Pleasant family had moved out of Acadia a few years ago. That's probably part of why she stopped coming—no family here to visit. Even still . . .

*There's got to be someone in town with a connection,* I said. *Some old friend who could contact her, or know how to get in touch with her family. They were from here. She loves Acadia.*

*Uhhh you know what they say*

*???*

*Lord help me I am never going back*

*That's just a song*

*LORD HELP ME BUT I AM NEVER EVER GOING BACK*

She sent a link a moment later, headlined A PLEASANT PLACE: THIRD ALBUM SEES COUNTRY DARLING LEAVING HER HEARTLAND BEHIND.

I frowned and typed, *That's just rumors.*

*Why would they print rumors?* Brit replied.

Dash chimed in then: *Why does anyone make anything up? For clicks and money*

Terrance too: *I know that's why I do literally everything*

And finally Flora: *I think it's a great idea Sophie!*

👍👍👍 ☺☺ ♡♡♡♡

I thought about my message to Megan all day at work. I regretted it—it was too short, I wrote it too fast. I should've drafted it, revised, proofread. I didn't feel like I captured it at all—what the band meant to me. How it was intrinsic to the town, to us as friends.

Dash and Brit were on the drum line. Side by side on their snares, what they did was precision, like surgery; it was deft and purposeful.

Terrance was in brass on trumpet. "Flashy," he would say with a grin, and it was true—the trumpets got the coolest solos.

I was in the woodwinds with Flora—her on flute and me on clarinet. My rented clarinet was the same one that Ciara had played—I made sure to ask for it special. It still had some of her stickers on the case, halfway peeled off. Ciara never loved band like I did, though, only did it because she didn't want to play a sport. For her, it was an obligation, a box to check, but for me . . . it was a community.

I loved it. Everything about it. The field on a Friday night, the crunch of the grass underfoot. The fancy uniforms for performances and competitions, the T-shirts and shorts for parades and afternoon games. I loved that moment when we got something on its feet, when we combined the music with the formations. I loved practicing through the neighborhood behind school, marching up and down the streets, past Flora's house and mine, past the library and the park.

We were the Pride of Acadia, and no one was prouder than me.

# nine

**Ciara:**

I saw a mullet today!!!!

                                **Sophie:**

                                !!!!!!!!!!!!!!!!!!!!!!!

**Ciara:**

It was incredible

11 out of 10

His hair was like . . . righteously thick

90s Dad would be SHOOK

                                **Sophie:**

                    Lolololol I can't believe he ever had one

**Ciara:**

Right?

Like not even just that it was a thing
But that it was HIS thing

**Sophie:**

90s Dad went on to land 00s Mom

**Ciara:**

I know

Their 90s hair looks combined

Would have been too powerful

**Sophie:**

It was def more like a half mullet by then

**Ciara:**

Yah

Business in the front, office worker's going away party
in the back

Like sheet cake and a card from Barb in Accounting in
the back

**Sophie:**

😆

I feel like a mullet spotting is good luck

**Ciara:**

Yes! Love it!

The new four leaf clover

It's decided

**Sophie:**

👍

# ten

I babysat for Cadence and Harper on Tuesday night.

Cadence decided she was going to "help" me take care of Harper for the evening, which mostly consisted of her giving a running commentary of Harper's thoughts and opinions.

Changing Harper's diaper: "She doesn't like that."

Filling Harper's tray: "She's extra hungry tonight."

Getting Harper in her pajamas: "She wants to wear the purple duck ones instead."

"Those are in the laundry."

Cadence's eyes were solemn: "She's okay with that."

The girls were in bed—wearing clean pajamas—and I was finally cleaning up from dinner when the back door opened slightly.

I turned at the sink, a pot in hand.

"This is me announcing myself," August said through the gap. "You know, in case you go into intruder alert mode."

I smiled. "No lasagna will die tonight on your behalf."

He stepped inside, and I turned back to the sink to finish scrubbing.

"What was for dinner?"

"Mac and cheese." I still had Harper's high chair tray to clean, all orange-crusted.

"The stove kind or the microwave kind?"

"The stove kind," I said, and suddenly he was right behind me, reaching past to grab a paper towel from the roll above the sink. He folded it up and stuck it briefly under the flow of water, and then went over to the high chair.

"That's like a hundred times better than the microwave kind, you know," he said as he began to scrub the tray. It would be faster to wash it in the sink, but it probably doesn't do much good to critique the nice thing someone is doing, so I just watched for a moment. He was wearing the same shirt he had on the night of the lasagna encounter, and I wondered briefly if it was his favorite shirt, or if he wore it specifically on Tuesdays, or if his closet was lined with rows of that exact shirt, like a cartoon character.

I went back to rinsing the pot.

"No leftovers tonight, sorry." I had horked down the rest of the mac and cheese while Cadence paused her description of Harper's inner monologue to tell me stories about dance class. She kept hopping out of her chair to show me moves, gravitating back to eat a forkful of food and then returning to the center of the kitchen, like a moth bouncing in and out of a porch light.

"No problem. Not hungry anyway."

I finished at the sink and watched August give the high chair one more swipe. He tossed the paper towel in the trash and then turned to me. For a moment we were both just standing there.

"Do you have, like . . . stuff to do?" he said finally. "While the girls are asleep?"

"Yeah, I usually go through Kyle and Heather's room. Try on all their clothes, roll around in their bed. That kind of thing."

He looked at me for a split second and then grinned. "I meant, like, watch TV or something."

"I usually do homework. But no homework now, so . . . maybe TV. Or a book or something." I looked at him. "What about you?"

"Probably just gonna hang out."

"Ah." *We could do that*, I almost said, before realizing it wasn't an invitation. Then I blinked. "Where's your room?"

"We're standing in it."

"This is the kitchen."

His eyes shone. "After hours, it's my room."

"What?"

He moved over to the window seat off the back of the kitchen, in the little alcove by the back door. It was a spot you'd sit in to take off your shoes, next to Kyle's boots and a pile of Cadence's sneakers.

For the first time, I noticed the quilt folded up on top of a pillow, shoved in the corner of the alcove. I watched as August sat, leaning against the wall and drawing his legs up.

I was still standing in the middle of the kitchen. "That's where you sleep?"

"Yeah."

"For real?"

"What?" I must have looked alarmed, because he shook his head. "It's fine. It's great, actually. It even opens up." He stood, picked up the cushion, and lifted the windowsill. "I can keep my stuff in there."

A folded pile of clothes lay inside—no duplicates of that shirt, which ruled out the cartoon-character theory—alongside a scrunched-up backpack, a few other odds and ends.

The window wasn't nearly long enough, though. August wasn't hugely tall—shorter than Terrance by an inch or two, and Dash by more. But he'd still have to curl up to sleep, under the pink-and-white quilt with rabbits on it.

"It's Cady's," he said, a little sheepish when he saw me looking. "She lent it to me."

This was a big deal, and I wasn't sure if he even realized it. Cadence wouldn't sleep under anything but the bunny quilt for a good six months or so. But that didn't factor at this moment.

"Why don't you sleep on the couch?" I said.

"I'd be in the way. No one needs the window."

"But it's a window."

"It's fine."

"It's . . . a window."

"Yes. And that's a door. That's a stove. Those are shoes."

I frowned. "We could work on the basement. Help Kyle out with it."

He was looking at me oddly. "You want to help do the basement?"

"Sure, how hard could it be? Putting up drywall. Nailing stuff. We could totally do that."

"Why would you care? You don't even know me."

I felt suddenly read. "Yeah, but . . . everyone's a neighbor in Acadia."

It was on the sign leading into town, in big stylized painted letters, like a 1950s postcard. When you left town, the other side read, YOU'RE ALWAYS WELCOME BACK.

He shook his head. "It's okay. It's just temporary."

"Yeah. About that. Heather said . . ."

"What?"

"I don't know, she made it sound like you would be around for school in the fall. Like it's not . . . as super temporary . . . as you made it sound."

Something in August's eyes shuttered. Glancing away, he said, "I mean, I might enroll. For the fall. If I'm still here." The way he said it sounded like a concession.

"Oh. Cool."

The back door rustled then. I wasn't even standing that close to August, but I felt compelled to move away as the door opened and Heather emerged.

She looked between us for a second before tossing her keys and her purse down on the kitchen table. "Well, hey there. How's it going?"

"Good," I said, too fast. "The girls are sleeping."

"Cady didn't give you any trouble about bedtime?"

"Nope. Perfect angels."

Heather snorted. "I wouldn't go that far, but I appreciate it." She set about paying me, and then she glanced at the clock on the wall, the one that made a different bird sound every hour on the hour. "Hey, the Yum Yum Shoppe's still open. If you guys hurry, you can get some ice cream." She grabbed the keys off the table and tossed them at August. "You can take my car."

He looked hesitant.

"Go. Live a little. Enjoy the sugar and fat while your bodies are still young and springy."

Heather was still pretty young and springy herself. She had been one of my mom's students. She still slipped up and called her "Mrs. Kemper" sometimes, despite all the instances my mom had said to call her by her first name. My parents had the Conlins over for dinner not long after they had moved in, and I remember Heather shaking her head and laughing when my mom offered her a drink: *I can't take* booze *from* Mrs. Kemper!

*Honey, if you're trying to make me feel positively ancient, it's working,* my mom had replied, and Heather, chastened but still laughing, took the beer.

Right now, she looked between August and me expectantly.

August glanced at me. "Do you want to—?"

"Yes." A little too quick on the draw. I coughed. "Yeah. Sure."

Heather winked at me as we headed out.

Terrance worked at the Yum Yum Shoppe. He and Brit had started there together, but according to Terrance, *Only one awesome person can work there at a time.* At least, that's what he had texted when Brit told the rest of the group about getting fired (*I didn't like it there* is how she put it in the chat, but we all knew what that meant).

*That's probably fair*, Brit had replied. *Since everyone else who works there uncategorically blows.*

*How do you blow categorically?* Terrance asked.

*Using your hand to assist your mouth*, Brit said. *It simulates greater depth.*

*BRITTANY. ELIZABETH. CARTER* was my contribution.

*It's just Brit, and you know it. My parents gave me half a name.*

*You should use your hand to assist your name*, Dash said, and Flora threatened to leave the chat.

Tonight I watched Terrance as the line at the Yum Yum Shoppe inched forward. He was entrenched behind the fudge case next to the cash register, both arms resting on top as he spoke to a woman with two little girls who were already clutching cones. I could hear him over the din:

"But you gotta try the new fudge, it's got these huge white chocolate chunks and, uh, what is it, Kim?"

"Heath bars," Kim supplied as she rang them up.

"Heath bars. Hands down best fudge I've ever had in my life. And I've tried every fudge here at least twelve times."

The woman huffed a laugh.

By the time we reached the register, three people had bought fudge.

"So they just have you stand here and upsell people?" August said.

Terrance grinned. "Sometimes I switch to cookies. They have this insane peanut butter cookie—"

"If you're gonna pitch us, you could at least give us a discount," I said.

"No discounts," Kim said flatly.

"You're the light of my life, Kim," Terrance replied. She didn't smile.

"You sure you don't want anything?" I glanced at August before taking my mint-chocolate-chip cone. He shook his head and dug into his pocket, pulling out his wallet.

"Don't do that," I said, handing my cone back to Terrance, who looked slightly bewildered, and reaching for my own money. But August had already handed a few bills over to Kim.

"Cookie or fudge, which one's better?" I said to Terrance.

"That's like asking a mom to choose between her kids," he replied, deadpan.

"Jesus Christ, give me both, then."

I handed them to August as Kim rang me up. "Enjoy."

"I said I wasn't hungry."

"I said not to pay for me."

"She's got you there," Terrance remarked, and then batted his eyes at Kim. "I'm going on break. Try not to miss me too much."

The three of us sat on the back steps to the building while we ate, and Terrance chatted amiably with August. A tiny part of me was irrationally annoyed that Terrance was crashing whatever this was—a date? Did it count as a date if Heather basically contrived it for me?—but I knew Terrance would be a good person for August to hang out with. Terrance could make friends with anyone. It was one of my favorite things about him—there wasn't a person he couldn't talk to, or an awkward silence he couldn't transform.

Despite saying he wasn't hungry, August tore through the fudge and cookie in record time. He handed the waxed paper packets back to me when he was done, and "Thanks for your trash" was on the tip of my tongue before I realized there was a piece of each remaining.

"Try them," he said. "They're good."

"It's the best fudge I've ever had," Terrance reminded us. "And I've tried every fudge on earth ninety-seven times."

He was ridiculous, but he was right. It was incredible.

"Is this place hiring?" August asked as I ate.

Terrance shook his head. "Nah. Not right now. They just hired. McDonald's might be, though, you should ask Flora."

August nodded. "I put in an application there. And at Pizza Hut."

"Somewhere'll take you," I said. "I heard someone say there was an opening at Dollar Depot."

"I'll look there too, thanks."

He and Terrance had exchanged numbers by the time Terrance

had to go back in, Terrance inviting August to the pickup football game he and Dash were playing in that weekend.

I was almost finished with my cone by the time Terrance went back to work, but I gave in to the temptation to stretch it out, holding the last pointy bit of it longer than I should, managing the drips that tipped over the jagged edges while August and I kept talking. He was sitting on the step below me, leaning back on his elbows so his face turned up whenever he looked my way.

I didn't know you could simultaneously find someone easy to talk to, and yet somehow be conscious of everything you're doing around them. Like how your body exists in space, and where your hands are in relation to theirs. August managed to inspire it. I couldn't tell if it was mutual. I wanted it to be.

Finally I had to finish the cone. It was soggy, and basically empty, but I ate it anyway. I wiped my hands on my shorts. We talked some more.

"Do you have a curfew?" he said eventually.

"Sort of? Not really. Like, I usually just go home." Maximum coolness.

"Mine is soon," he said, and he sounded like maybe he regretted it, but then again maybe I was just imagining it.

"This was Heather's idea, though, so I feel like there might be a bit of leeway there."

He smiled, and I was almost certain there was a little regret when he said, "Probably shouldn't risk it."

*  *  *

I couldn't get to sleep that night, and sometimes when I couldn't sleep, I thought about my colleges. I had created a broad list at the beginning of junior year, as *The College Collective* had advised, and had slowly whittled it down over the course of the year, after a lot of research and consideration.

Each one of them was a possibility, a different fork in the road. Each one had the potential to make me into a different person.

I stared at the ceiling and thought about them in groups first. Community colleges. State schools. Private universities.

Then I ranked them from likelihood of my acceptance, which coincidentally was the same order as when I ranked them in likelihood I'd be able to afford going.

Then I ranked them as distance from Acadia.

I squeezed my eyes shut. I remember Ciara getting her scholarship packet from Tufts. She had already been accepted to a few places, had already gotten a great scholarship offer from the University of Illinois. She would have to make a decision. But when that stuff from Tufts arrived . . . I knew it wasn't really a decision at all.

I remember googling the distance between Acadia and Boston. It was a sixteen-hour drive. If I needed her, there would be sixteen hours' worth of road between us.

I had spent my whole life with her sleeping in the bed across from mine. Until suddenly she wasn't.

There was Skype, though, and phone calls.

There were texts.

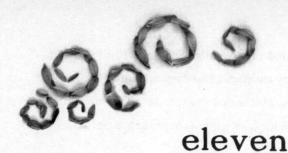

# eleven

**Sophie:**

Do you ever feel like you have two lives now?

**Ciara:**

Girl it is LATE

Shouldn't you be sleeping?

**Sophie:**

Shouldn't YOU?

**Ciara:**

I'm in college, it's allowed

I woke up at noon and ate cocoa puffs for lunch

Why are you still up? Everything okay?

**Sophie:**

Yeah just thinking

Do you ever feel like you have two lives?

Is that what happens when you leave home?

**Ciara:**

Hmmmmm

No

Same life. Just relocated

**Sophie:**

But you belong to both places

Or do you not feel like that anymore?

Like home isn't home

**Ciara:**

These are deep questions for this time of night

**Sophie:**

It's this time of night that makes me think them, lol

**Ciara:**  /

Well let me think

I would say home is still home

But this is home too

So like two homes, but one life

**Sophie:**

Do you like it better there though? Is one home

better than the other?

**Ciara:**

It's different

I like it a lot

But that doesn't mean I like Acadia any less

After all, you're there
☺

**Sophie:**

And mom and dad

**Ciara:**

And mom and dad too
Now get some sleep!!

**Sophie:**

Okaaaaaay

**Ciara:**

Miss you lots

**Sophie:**

♡ ♡ ♡

# twelve

I sent a message off to the chat the next day: *Let's meet at TZ2. Want to talk about fundraising stuff.* I wanted everyone there at one time, ready to hear my plan.

Brit, Dash, and Flora were seated on the lumpy old couch, Terrance and August in a couple of plastic lawn chairs. August hadn't been inducted into the WHERE WILL YOU SPEND ETERNITY group chat yet, but I texted him separately—*Want to hang out at Terrance and Dash's house?*

So he had his first introduction to Teen Zone 2—the pole shed tucked in one corner of the Cunninghams' backyard, the fence on one side, a tall elm on the other. It was pretty decently sized, red with a white garage-style door that we left up when the weather was good.

"Why do you call it Teen Zone Two?" August asked.

"Teen Zone One was already taken," Brit replied.

"It's not Teen Zone One, it's just Teen Zone, period," I said.

"Like how it's not *The Fast and the Furious One*," Terrance supplied.

Dash nodded. "Or how it's not *Star Wars One*."

"No, it's definitely called *Star Wars One*," Brit said, just to be contrary.

"It's named in tribute to the youth corner at the library," I told August.

"*Star Wars One?*"

"Teen Zone Two."

"That makes more sense."

"Nothing about this makes sense." Brit looked at me. "Why are we here again?"

"Okay." I moved to stand in front of the open door to address everyone. "I'm guessing you've all seen my idea for fall festival."

Terrance nodded. "We build giant corn effigies and people pay to burn them in an empty field."

"That's not—"

"I love it. Sold. Fuck yeah," Brit said.

"About Megan Pleasant," I said. "About how we should invite her to play a fundraising concert at Fall Fest."

Brit made a face. "Oh, that idea."

"Why don't we just propose it to the booster club?" Terrance asked.

"Because I think this would be a fun thing for MPASFC to take charge of. We could bring it to the booster club if we manage to get a lead. And if not, then we'll just . . . pretend it never happened."

"Sophie's super good at that," Brit said to August, and I threw a pen at her.

"What's your plan?" Dash asked, kind enough to stay on topic.

"Well, it has multiple steps," I began.

"Of course it does," Brit interjected.

"I made a presentation." I went over and opened up my dad's laptop where it sat atop the Ping-Pong table.

"Nooooo! Sophie!" Brit threw the pen back at me. "This is summer vacation! No PowerPoints, geez."

"But . . . it highlights all my points."

"Condense your points."

I sighed and closed the laptop.

"Okay. A multipronged approach. First, social media outreach—I already started that. We contact Megan on every social network possible. We don't spam—like we don't want to be obnoxious—but we *politely* mention our situation and ask her if she'd be interested in coming to town. And we talk about how important it is to us to go to the parade, and how great it is for Acadia, and how much we love her."

"This is so many words," Brit said.

"The PowerPoint has visuals; it would make it easier to remember—"

She waved a hand. "Second prong."

"We look for local contacts. She grew up here. Her family moved away, but they must still keep in touch with people. Someone here might be able to get in contact with her, or her parents. Someone's gotta know something."

"So what?" Terrance said. "We go out and interrogate people for info on the Pleasant family?"

"We go out and *politely ask around*."

"You've said 'politely' twice now," Brit said.

"Yeah. For your benefit."

She looked scandalized. "I'm a delight."

"Uh-huh."

"Third prong," Dash prompted.

"Megan is playing at the Illinois State Fair this summer. We could get tickets and go, and like make signs or something, try to get her attention. Especially if we can drum up some buzz online, she might notice us, and maybe we could try to convince her in person."

"This all sounds like a lot of work," Brit said.

"Everything worth having is worth working for," I replied, and she groaned.

"Oh God, what's next? 'Good hustle'? 'Let's light a fire under them'? You sound just like my dad."

"Who do you think I got it from?"

"I mean, definitely not your own dad. He's too chill to be spewing bullshit like that."

We sat around the garage after that, after everyone added Megan Pleasant on every social network we could think of, and I read them a new email I had drafted as an example for what we're going for in our messages to Megan.

Finally Brit declared, "Enough already. Let's do something."

I frowned. "This is something."

"Something *fun*. No one has to work for once. Let's go somewhere."

"How about a movie?" August suggested. He had been pretty quiet throughout the brainstorming session. "Is there a movie theater around here?"

"The Movie Dome, in Fall Creek," Dash said.

"Six majestic screens," Terrance said. "Bring your own candy, because the shit in the case is as old as we are. No one's paying five dollars for some ancient-ass Twizzlers Twerpz."

"Do they still make those?" August said.

"They definitely do not," Terrance replied.

August smiled. "How far is it?"

"Like half an hour," Flora replied.

He looked surprised, just briefly, but Brit caught it.

"What, were you lousy with movie theaters back home? Was there one on every corner?"

"Yes," he said solemnly. "There were ten movie theaters per square block."

"But seriously, does living here totally wig you out?" Brit asked. "Does everything seem so far away?"

"I don't live here," he replied. "Just visiting."

Brit opened her mouth to respond, but before she could, Flora interrupted—gently—with movie options.

We found one that we all agreed on, and only realized there was a problem when we reached the Cutlass—it only seated five.

"Just squish in," August said. "We can fit four in the back."

Brit shook her head. "Not happening. Who stays?"

"I can," Flora said.

"I'll stay too," Terrance volunteered.

Flora frowned. "Well, then I'll go if you're not gonna."

"But who will keep me company?"

Flora looked at Brit, who looked at me.

I knew I couldn't borrow my dad's car at the moment. "I'll stay," I said. "You guys go."

"No, because you'll just update your sad PowerPoint and compose tweets to Megan Pleasant, and that thought is too depressing for me to handle on a fine afternoon like this. Flora and Terrance stay. This is a seniors-only movie excursion."

We weren't seniors yet, technically, according to *The College Collective*. This summer was labeled JUNIOR YEAR, JUNE–AUGUST, after all. We were in the *eve of senior year*.

I didn't point that out, though, and Flora just sighed. "Fine."

So we drove to Fall Creek and went to the Movie Dome.

We got seats toward the middle of the auditorium. Brit held back and let August go into the row first, so the seating order went August, me, Brit, and then Dash. When I looked over at Brit, she winked at me just like Heather had before we went to the Yum Yum Shoppe.

"Look at this," she said, throwing herself down into her seat. "Just like a double date." Then she popped right back up. "Who wants popcorn?"

We had already stopped at a gas station and loaded up on candy, but I wouldn't say no to movie theater popcorn. "Get the refill one and we can all share it."

"Excellent," Brit said. "I will need money for popcorn."

I rolled my eyes and fished out some money. Brit grabbed it and ushered Dash out of his seat. "We'll be back!" she said, reaching up to throw her arm around Dash's shoulders once they got to the aisle. Dash snaked his arm around her waist, and they matched their steps as they made their way back down the stairs toward the exit, heads bent toward each other in conversation.

August watched them go and then glanced at me.

"Are they dating?" he said.

"Dash and Brit? God no. He's—" I stopped myself. I wasn't exactly sure of the logistics of it—being out—but I knew it meant he told people, instead of people telling others on his behalf. "He's seeing somebody," I finished. "And Brit . . ." Is into herself? Into everyone? Into no one? I honestly couldn't tell sometimes. She had never had a long-term anything before, but occasionally she would disappear with people at parties and come back with color high in her cheeks, her hair mussed. She would have hickeys sometimes and not bother to hide them, but she never really went on *date* dates, or if she did, she never told me about them.

"Brit does her own thing," I finished.

It was quiet for a moment, and I thought about last night, the easy conversation outside the Yum Yum Shoppe.

"Would it be so bad, though?" I said. "If this were a double date?"

"Well, apparently Dash and Brit aren't happening, so half of it would already be null."

"What about the us half?"

It was very quiet now, aside from the voiceover of the commercial playing on screen, and the squawk of some little kids a few rows in front of us, fighting over a pack of Sour Patch Kids.

"You . . . seem really nice," August said after a moment.

"Oh, great. That's a great start," I said, and smiled because sometimes that's all you really can do—just smile because if something is going to suck, it might as well be funny. "Never mind."

"No, I mean . . . it's not you, you're—" He paused. "I just. I'm not trying to start any kind of . . . us . . . stuff. With anyone."

"It's fine." I opened the Twizzlers I had brought and pulled one out, telling myself that I felt absolutely no steady, sinking feeling inside. It was all very chill and unaffecting. "I always used to bite the ends off these and make straws—did you ever do that?"

He shook his head, and it was quiet once more. The smaller kid in front had succeeded in wresting the candy away from his brother.

When August spoke again, his voice was odd. Higher, and maybe the slightest bit unsure. "I could use a friend, though." When

I looked over at him, his eyes were fixed on the movie screen. "If you were . . . okay with that. That would be cool. Probably."

I nodded, after a beat. "I could do that." I took a bite of Twizzler and chewed, watching the corner of his mouth tick up when I added, "Probably."

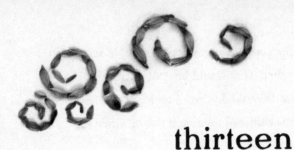

# thirteen

**Sophie:**

Did you like Ravi first or did he like you first?

Or was it mutual liking?

**Ciara:**

Mutual liking, I think

**Sophie:**

That's lucky

**Ciara:**

Oh yeah?

**Sophie:**

Yeah

Right?

Like what are the chances?

**Ciara:**

Uhhhhh pretty high?

I'M AMAZING REMEMBER

Or have you forgotten in my absence?

> **Sophie:**
>
> Lolol yeah
>
> I just mean it seems like a lot of stuff has to like
>
> Line up
>
> In order for you and the person you like to both
>
> like each other at the same time
>
> And the same amount

**Ciara:**

Maybe it's not always the same amount at first

Maybe someone grows to meet the other

I don't know though

I'm not an expert

I just got lucky with Ravi

> **Sophie:**
>
> Not really

**Ciara:**

Heyyy!

> **Sophie:**
>
> I just mean he's the lucky one

**Ciara:**

Bawwwww

                              **Sophie:**

    We should go to the Movie Dome when you're back

**Ciara:**

Don't you wonder why they called it that?

It's not like there's imax or anything

Nothing about that place is domed

                              **Sophie:**

                    What would you call it?

**Ciara:**

The Movie Pit

                              **Sophie:**

                    That's so much better

**Ciara:**

What can I say, it's a gift

☺

# fourteen

People got together at Jake Weaver's house on Thursday night. It was outside of town, and I had to borrow my dad's car to get us there, seeing as we now surpassed carpool capacity in the Cutlass.

"Now where are we going?" Dad said when I asked, looking up from his paper. He and my mom did crossword puzzles like they were an Olympic sport.

"*I* am going to Jake Weaver's house."

He raised an eyebrow. "Do we know Jake Weaver?"

"He's from school."

"Oh, from school. That clears it up. Take my keys. And my debit card too, let's give Jake Weaver from school free rein over our bank account."

I laughed. "You know his mom. She has the bakeshop? By Dr. Aniz?"

"Oh, Sally?"

"I guess?"

"Sammy." He snapped his fingers. "Patty. Patty Weaver. Oh yeah. She makes a great lemon tart."

"I heard she also makes responsible children."

My dad grinned. "Be careful on the road."

I jumped up and went for the keys by the door.

"Soph?" he called as I started out.

"Super careful!" I said, looking back. He nodded and returned to his crossword.

"'Nine letters, cryptid,'" he murmured.

Brit and Flora met me outside, Flora in even more improbable shoes than last time. They made her almost as tall as Brit, which I knew Brit hated.

*Height is the only thing I have over her*, she said once. *She's cuter and nicer and smarter and people like her more and her hair is shinier. If I can't be taller, I have nothing.*

*You definitely run faster than her.*

*That doesn't count. I run faster than everyone.*

I texted August—because we did that more often now, texting casually, like friends—and he emerged from the Conlins' house, two doors down, and gave us a wave.

"So is this a permanent thing?" Brit said as he approached. "We're officially adopting him now?"

"I think he's nice," Flora said.

"Shocking," Brit replied, and got in the front seat.

We split up inside Jake's house, pulled in several different directions as a guy from the football team waved Brit down, and Flora spotted some junior girls. August and I wandered a bit, eventually making our way to the kitchen to get drinks.

A group of guys was gathered there in a rough circle. They were, apparently, discussing how to crush a can on your forehead.

"You have to squeeze it first," the guy nearest us said.

"Nah, that's like pre-crushing. That's cheating."

"You have to! Or else it won't do it!" he insisted.

"I got this, I got it." One guy finished off his drink quickly. His name was Dylan, and he was a sophomore in the brass section. All eyes were on him as he held up the can for the group to see and then raised it dramatically in the air and aimed it toward himself.

Next to me, August shifted forward. "Hey, maybe don't—"

Dylan slammed the can straight at the center of his forehead, and then let out a yelp, the decidedly uncrushed can falling to the ground.

The group erupted as Dylan clutched his head:

"Wooooooow."

"I told you, you have to crush it first!"

"Coach Junior," someone said, and they all cracked up.

"Fuck you guys," Dylan said, face angled downward, still holding his head.

"No, that was a Coach Junior right there, even you have to admit it."

August cut past me as the guys kept talking, went to the fridge, and got out a couple of cans of soda. Dylan had shuffled to the side.

I watched as August moved toward him. He pulled Dylan's hand away from his head—Dylan, who was blinking rapidly, let him—inspected his forehead for a moment, and then held the soda up against it. "Just hold it there."

Dylan looked confused—pained and probably drunk. "To crush it?"

"In case it swells up," August said.

"It's gonna swell?"

"Not if you hold that there."

Dylan nodded dutifully, and August returned to me.

"Who's Coach Junior?" he said, handing me the other soda.

The guy nearest us heard him. "The coach's kid? He was a few years ahead of us. He tried to kill himself senior year by jumping off a garage. All he did was break his legs."

August frowned. "Is that . . . funny?"

"It's funny 'cause he lived. If he died we wouldn't joke about it, obviously."

"Obviously," August repeated.

The guy speaking was named Troy Fowler. I had been all through school with him. I still remembered one time he missed a week of school in fourth grade to go with his mom to visit family in Michigan. When he came back to class the next week, all he could talk about was an accident they had seen on the interstate driving up there. Two semitrucks had crashed into each other, and multiple cars piled up behind.

"The trucks crashed together, and then the cars behind them crashed into trucks, just *bam bam bam*"—he had smacked his hands together—"*ka-blam!*"

There were fire trucks and ambulances and a helicopter apparently, and Troy and his mom were in terrible traffic, even coming the opposite way, backed up for miles as people slowed to look while they passed. The firefighters had held up sheets around some of the crashed cars.

Dash had listened to this account with a frown, his brow furrowed. "Why?"

"So people couldn't see the dead bodies when they pulled them out." Troy slapped his hands together again for emphasis. "*Ka-blam*, remember?"

Right now he blinked at August. "No, he's totally fine. So it's funny. He legit thought he was going to end it jumping like eight feet. It was idiotic."

August opened his mouth to speak, but I had had enough of Troy Fowler, so I tugged on August's arm.

"Want to go outside?"

We ended up on the back porch. I shot off a quick text to WWYSE:

*We're in the back*

It was quiet between August and me. I could hear Troy laughing inside. That loud bray. *It was idiotic.*

"He wasn't trying to kill himself," I said.

"Hm?"

"Coach Junior."

"Oh."

"And that's not even—it's a stupid nickname. His name is Luke. And he was high. Some guys at a party slipped him something. He was totally out of it. Thought he could fly or something."

"You know him?"

I nodded. "Yeah. Brit's brother."

Luke was probably my first crush, though I wouldn't have known to call it that at the time. Maybe he was Ciara's too—when we were little he had pegs on the back of his bike and she used to stand on them, holding Luke's shoulders as he pedaled fast up and down the street, her hair flowing out behind her, a huge grin on her face. She'd say I was too little to ride, but I think she just liked keeping it as something between them.

The breaks in Luke's legs were bad, and he had to have a couple of operations, had to go back and forth to Effingham for physical therapy. He missed the last few months of his senior year, and deferred his acceptance to University of Illinois. He never ended up going.

He got around fine now, but whatever plans he had before—college, everything—were derailed, and he couldn't seem to find his way back to them.

We were in eighth grade when it happened. I remember Brit's eyes, bright and red-rimmed, telling me it was Tanner Barnes and his friends who spiked Luke's drink as a joke.

"He should be in jail," she said, voice choked with anger and tears. "He should get arrested for this. He should have to pay."

This was the origin of Brit's thesis statement for the next four years—making Tanner Barnes pay. Tanner, who was Acadia's number one track-and-field star, ranked at the state level. Had scholarship offers from multiple schools. Was close to getting fast enough in the 100 meter to qualify for the Olympic Trials.

*He wanted to make Luke look stupid. He wanted to humiliate him. So I'm going to humiliate him right back. One day I'm going to race him, and I'm going to beat him.*

*How will that humiliate him?*

*Because he's an egotistical asshole. So I'm going to do better than he ever did.*

I thought of that night outside McDonald's—*What do you want most in the world?* I didn't need to ask Brit, because I already knew.

"That's terrible," August said.

"Yeah." I fiddled with the tab on the top of my soda, and then it was quiet. "So . . ." I wanted to lighten things up. "Anyway. Anything new with you?"

He smiled a little. "I got a job."

"Oh yeah?"

A nod. "Dollar Depot."

"Nice."

"I think my ability to lift thirty pounds really sealed the deal," he said. "Also my awesome personality."

"Can't forget that."

It was quiet again.

"Have you done any social media outreach?" The Megan Pleasant plan was never far from my mind.

He made a funny face. "I didn't think I was really in on the whole . . . Megan thing. I'm not in the band."

"Well, we could use your help no matter what. But you should try out." A pause. "You know, like in case you're still here for the fall."

"Maybe."

"We start back up soon, for the Fourth of July parade. You could audition for Ms. Hill."

"I don't have a sax here."

"You can rent one."

He gave a noncommittal "Mm."

I paused, and then spoke carefully: "They have scholarships and stuff, too. To cover the rentals and all that. It comes out of the big fund."

"Thought you needed the big fund to get to the parade."

"Well, when we get Megan here, the big fund will be pretty big, right?" I nudged him with my elbow. "At least try out. They'll have rookie camp for the new students—mostly freshmen and stuff, but also people from other grades who want to join, so you could get all caught up."

He nodded. "Maybe."

The back door flew open then, and Brit burst through, Dash following at a more sedate pace.

"Are we interrupting?" Brit said, plopping down next to me and forcing me into August's side. "I hope not."

"We were just talking about band stuff," I said.

"Sexy," Brit replied, and then leaned across me to August. "You should see Soph on the clarinet. It's a reed instrument. Lots of tongue action." She winked, hugely. "Just think of the possibilities. Connect the dots. Between that. And"—she gestured vaguely at his crotch—"all that."

"*Brit.*"

"Sophie." Her eyes were wide and guileless.

"You don't get how a reed instrument works" is all I could say.

"Of course not, I play snare drum."

I glanced at August, but he just looked amused. "Is my dick the clarinet? Or the reed? We're working on a really different size scale either way."

"What are we talking about?" Terrance asked, pushing through the door with a plastic cup in each hand, Flora right behind him.

"Clarinet-size dick," Dash replied as Terrance handed him one of the cups.

"Oh geez, can you imagine?" Terrance said.

"I don't have to imagine," August said. "That's pretty much the situation down there."

Flora's eyes widened.

"He's joking," I told her.

"Dead serious. It's a total liability."

Flora started laughing, and then waving her hands in the air as if to get our attention, and then laughing some more.

"What?"

"Just th-th-thinking—" she stuttered, shoulders shaking. "You'd

101

have to use—one of those long plastic bags—that newspapers come in—as a—When you—To protect—" She flapped her hands. "For sex!"

"Flora Maria Feliciano, how dare you," Brit said as Flora dabbed tears from the corners of her eyes.

"Everyone else gets to make jokes! I don't get to make jokes?"

"No, it was good," Terrance said. "I like where your head is at."

"We know where August's head is at," Flora said, and clapped a hand to her mouth, withdrawing it only momentarily to screech: "His knees!"

It was a while before the resulting group reaction died down.

"Okay," Brit said finally. "All right. I think it's time we all get to know August a little better."

"Everyone says that when they find out about my clarinet-size dick."

Brit grinned. "Tell us all about yourself, August Your-last-name."

She didn't remember the last party: *Shaw. Conlin. Hm.*

"What do you want to know?"

"What's your deal? Why are you here?"

"What kind of a question is that?" Dash said. "Why are any of us here?"

"Yeah, like what's my cosmic mission?" August said.

"Why are you here in Acadia? With us, on this porch right now?" Brit replied.

"I mean, I'm on the porch because I followed Sophie."

"We're all here on the porch because we followed Sophie some-where at some point in our lives, but like why are you here in town?" she pressed.

"What do you think of Acadia so far?" Flora added, and I silently thanked her. Sometimes she was the best at wresting control of a conversation from Brit, even if it wasn't always intentional.

"It's fine," August replied evenly.

"You can be a little more enthusiastic," I said.

"It's . . ." He squinted up at the sky like he was consulting with it on an answer, before settling on "Unique?"

That was about on par with *You seem really nice.*

"You know, it's actually not unique at all," Brit said. "There's another Acadia in California."

I nodded. "We found it online. They're trying to put their Acadia High School on the historical register. It's that nice."

"Sometimes we pretend what it would be like if we went to the other Acadia High School," Flora said.

It had become a thing—our lives were better at Other Acadia.

Or at least they were different. *It might not solve our problems, but it could give us new ones,* Flora would say. No one loved the Other Acadia fantasy more than she did.

"What's it like there?" August asked.

"Just like here," Flora replied. "Except everyone has exactly what they want."

"For real, what's your deal, though?" Brit reached across me to poke August in the arm.

He didn't respond, just got to his feet and nodded toward Terrance. "You want to introduce me to some people?"

"I don't know any other people," Terrance replied, deadpan. "That's the only reason I'm here." But he stood too and followed August inside.

Brit leaned in to me when they left. "Don't worry. I'm gonna wingman the shit out of this for you. This right here—still laying the foundation."

"Thanks, but I'm good."

"You are," she replied. "Too good."

# fifteen

Flora and I ended up standing on my front lawn with August at the end of the evening, having left Terrance and Dash behind to deal with Brit.

"Sleepover?" Flora said, when August had retreated to the Conlins' house. I nodded.

I stopped at home and said hi to my folks, changed into my pajamas, then headed next door. The front door was open—Mrs. Feliciano was on the couch, watching TV, her phone pressed to her ear. She waved when she saw me, then gestured in the direction of Flora's room.

The bathroom door was shut, light seeping out from underneath when I stepped into the hallway, so I headed into Flora's room.

She was an only child—never had to share a room. Even Brit

and Luke shared when they were little, before Luke got the basement. And I had shared with Ciara almost my whole life, until she went off to college.

I remember watching Ciara taking her clothes out of the closet, piling them into a suitcase. *Isn't it nice you'll have more space? You can spread out.*

I didn't want to spread out, if it meant filling the places she had existed before.

I sat on Flora's bed while she was in the bathroom and fussed with my phone for a moment. I hadn't messaged Megan yet today, so I did that quickly—*Hi, this is Sophie from the Marching Pride of Acadia and we would love to host you for our annual fall festival* . . .

Then I set my phone aside.

Flora's room was a little like a time capsule. It had the same wallpaper runner around the top of the room as it did when we were little kids: cartoon sheep jumping over fences, rolling green hills behind them. Newer interests were layered over older ones—hand-painted pictures and drawings were partially obscured by magazine tear-outs of pop stars, which were partially obscured by movie posters.

On the shelves by her window were stacks of books, piled high and color-coordinated. One shelf was dedicated to Flora's miniatures—a tiny café, a little bookstore, a bakery with shelves filled with tiny cakes and macarons and teacups.

It's not exactly right to say I *worried* about Flora. But she was just so . . . soft sometimes, so unguarded. We begged our moms for these knockoff American Girl dolls when we were younger and Flora still had hers, all of its clothes and accessories. Sometimes— rarely, but still, every now and then—I would come over and it would have a new hairstyle, or be wearing a different jacket.

There's no expiration date on that kind of stuff, not a spoken one, anyway, but whatever it was that crushed it out of the rest of us—made Terrance and Dash put down their Power Rangers action figures and never pick them back up again—I don't think it had happened to Flora yet.

And part of me hoped it never would. But part of me just . . . worried, sometimes. I worried about what she would do next year if Brit and I weren't around anymore, if we both went away to school.

I worried about what Brit would do, if she and I went away to different schools.

I worried a lot, basically. And it was easiest to worry in times like this, when it was quiet, when I was alone, when there was nothing to distract me.

I picked up my phone again and checked my notifications, just in case Megan had somehow miraculously replied in the last two minutes. She hadn't.

I tried to think of happier things. The last time Brit and I were over here, Flora was trying to do a makeup tutorial from YouTube with Brit as her subject. Flora loved makeup tutorials. Makeup in general. We had pooled our money and gotten her this palette she really wanted for her birthday.

Brit and Flora sat on Flora's bed, Brit with her eyes closed as

Flora brushed and swiped and blended. She had been trying to fill in Brit's eyebrows when I finally looked up and couldn't help but sputter a laugh.

"What are you doing?"

Brit's eyes sprang open. "What? What did you do?"

"It might be a *little* much, but they said you have to go in with a strong hand," Flora said. "I'll fix it."

"Lemme see."

"No, I want to finish," Flora said, and then grinned at me when Brit shut her eyes.

Instead of taking stuff off, Flora doubled down with the eyebrow filler, and drew Brit's eyebrows approximately three times their normal thickness.

I had to bite the inside of my cheek to keep from laughing.

When she finally handed Brit the mirror, Brit let out an unholy yelp, and Flora burst into hysterical laughter.

"What the hell? WHAT THE HELL, FLORA?"

"I knew I couldn't fix them," she said. "So I made it funny instead."

"This is not—You are so—" Brit blustered, but Flora just laughed harder, throwing herself back against the pillows, tears in her eyes.

"You—look—so—ridiculous—" she wheezed, and I doubled over.

"I HATE BOTH OF YOU."

The Brit Rule stood as follows: when she said she hated something, it usually meant that she loved it. It was the rule of opposites. But in this moment, she may have actually meant hate.

Until she dropped the mirror on the comforter and began tickling Flora.

"No." Flora beat her fists out helplessly, laughing harder. "No, I can't, I'm gonna pee—"

"Pee, then," Brit said, still tickling. "Me and my eyebrows will judge you."

"You're nothing but eyebrows," Flora gasped. "You and your eyebrows—are the same thing—You are—your eyebrows—"

I smiled to myself now, alone in Flora's room, with the memory of them both laughing.

"What did you talk about with August tonight?" Flora said, when we were both in bed.

"Not much," I said. "Band stuff mostly."

"Hmm," she replied, a little too knowingly.

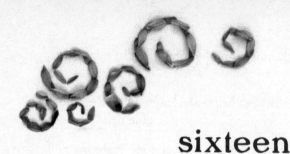

# sixteen

Kyle showed up in my checkout lane at Safeway a few days later with a gallon of milk, a big package of diapers, some odds and ends.

"Funny how she just keeps going through 'em," he said as I swiped the diapers. I glanced up at him with a smile and was surprised to see the same tilt to his grin that August had. I had never noticed it before. Or I guess I had never known to look.

I looked away as I reached for a box of Cheerios.

"So, uh, how's August doing?"

"Good. I think? I hope." He scratched his chin absently. "I don't know, I've been working a lot. I think you've probably gotten to spend more time with him than I have." He smiled again. Brit always commented how hot he was, which made me uncomfortable because I thought of him as like a cool older brother/young uncle type. But objectively speaking, Kyle was hot in a way like he could play a too-old high schooler on a supernatural-themed TV show, or the action hero's best friend who gets blown up in a war movie. "He's talked about you, you know. Sophie this and Sophie that."

"Good things?"

"Doesn't get better than this and that, does it? That's top-shelf stuff right there."

I finished ringing up and started bagging while Kyle ran his card.

"So . . . he's going to be staying, then? Like for school and everything?"

Kyle glanced up, nodded. "Yeah, looks like it. With the girls and everything, you know, we wanted to be careful—bringing a stranger into the house and all that, but—Not that he's—" He looked flustered. "Just . . . you know. But he's great, he's a great kid. We love having him around. These last few weeks have been really cool, getting to know him."

"So you didn't . . . ?"

"Sorry?"

"Know him."

He looked away. "We didn't grow up together, no. Different, uh, different dads. I lived with my dad and stepmom here; he lived with our mom in Missouri. I wasn't . . . close with her at all. I didn't really know her either."

*What happened to her?* I didn't feel it was fair to ask, but I was desperate to know. Instead, I handed Kyle his receipt.

"Say hi to everyone for me."

"You got it. Have a good one, Soph." He collected his bags, and then he was gone.


Dash worked at Safeway too. We had both started there in junior year—he was saving for the Cutlass, and I was just saving.

Today he finished up half an hour after I did, but I hung around and waited for him, sitting outside on one of the concrete parking space bumpers and finishing off a half-priced deli sandwich.

Sometimes Dash and I just went driving. He liked to drive out past Acadia, out into the cornfields where everything was flat and the sky seemed impossibly wide. We'd see the crops change over time—green stalks, growing taller and thicker, then drying out, turning to that light tan color. Then cut down to nothing. The ground looked a bit like a desert after that—flat and brown and expansive. Then it would start all over again.

Brit would complain—*It's just corn on corn on corn, it's boring*—but I liked the rows. The order. The ritual.

Dash was my favorite person to be quiet with. In the same way Terrance was an easy talker, Dash was great at comfortable silence. I never felt pressure around him, like I had to say something. Like he expected anything from me.

It was on one of our drives this past spring when Dash had adjusted his grip on the steering wheel and said, "So."

There was a pause, but I knew he would follow it up with something. Dash took his time—always had. He was thoughtful and deliberate in a way that I wish I could be. I don't think he had ever said something he hadn't meant to.

He had spoken, eventually: "I met somebody. Online."

"Yeah?"

"Uh-huh. He goes to school in Indianapolis." Another pause. "We've been talking."

"Nice," I said. "About what?"

One corner of his mouth lifted. "Just talking." Silence. "Like how Terrance and Mia are talking."

Terrance had been very into Mia Reyes at that time. It would later end after they went to the spring dance together. Apparently she decided that Terrance's dance moves were just too much for her to handle. Or at least, that's what he told us.

"Oh," I said to Dash. "Cool." A pause. "What's he like?"

"Smart," Dash said, with a smile that I hadn't seen before—something small, private. "Funny."

"Good."

"Yeah?"

"Yeah, I mean. If he were stupid and humorless, there would be way less stuff to talk about." I glanced over at him. "Less stuff to like, right?"

His smile grew. "Right."

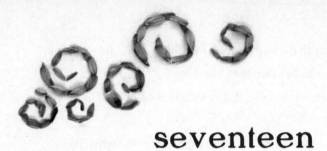

# seventeen

I tried, the next week, in between work and the library and baby-sitting, to rally interest in my Megan Pleasant project. I sent reminders out to WWYSE. I proposed information-gathering sessions that no one seemed to be available for.

Terrance shot me a list of ideas, but I knew he was only humoring me as the MPASFC's vice president.

Brit and I were biking to Teen Zone 2 one afternoon, and I couldn't help but bring it up.

"No one is on board with my Megan project. No one cares."

She looked over at me, pedaling with her hands off the handlebars. I didn't have the balance for that. "Translation: no one cares as much as you do. It's not our fault you care about shit like fifty times harder than the average person."

"I just . . . really want to do this. For all of us."

"There are other ways to raise money. Trust the booster club. There's still like six months to go, and they managed to get money for the Macy's parade back in the day."

"That's different. The band is bigger now, it's way more money, and also inflation and stuff—"

"Sophie. It's summer. Okay? Can we just . . . enjoy summer? Just for a little bit?"

I frowned. Brit might have been a little bit right. "Yeah. Okay."

"Say it like you mean it."

"Don't push it."

I went about ten minutes without talking about it.

Terrance was already at Teen Zone 2 when we arrived, and to my surprise, August was with him. They were playing Ping-Pong on the old table, which had a net at one point, but was now sadly lacking. Flora had drawn cartoon faces on each side of the paddles a while ago—happy on one side, frowning on the other.

"I play winner," Brit said, dropping her bag on the couch. She was supposedly starting a new job tonight, at Pizza Hut.

"Uh-uh," Terrance said. "We're doing a tournament."

"You can't do a tournament with two people."

"Can so."

August missed the next point, and then a few more, before surrendering his paddle to Brit. She held it up to her face so the happy side was out—a big half-circle smile and squiggly eyes.

"Thanks, friend!" she said in a creepy voice.

"No problem. Thanks for inspiring my nightmares."

He took a seat on the couch, a stretch of space between us.

"How's the Megan project going?" he said.

"Nooooo." Brit groaned. "We just decided to chill on the Megan Pleasant thing for a little bit."

"Technically *you* decided to chill on it," I said.

"You said we could enjoy summer!"

"We can do both." I looked at August. "We just need to gain some momentum."

"Do you really think you can get her to come?"

"For sure. It's not like it's some random town. It's *her* town. She loves Acadia."

"*Loved* Acadia," Brit corrected. "Past tense."

"You make it sound like she's dead," August said.

"Yeah, she definitely is." Brit backhanded the ball, and Terrance missed. "That's what all this is about. We're trying to track down her ghostly specter. Barring that, Megan Pleasant's hologram is gonna play the fall festival."

"I'm just saying, you said it in like a cryptic way."

"Aren't all specters ghostly?" Terrance asked, retrieving the ball.

"She's not dead," I told August.

"She just hates Acadia," Brit added, and easily returned Terrance's serve.

"She doesn't *hate* it. All that stuff has been super exaggerated."

"What stuff?" August asked.

"Well." Brit got another point off Terrance and put her paddle down while he went to collect the ball. She always said that celebrity gossip was stupid, but at the same time, Brit enjoyed other people's drama inherently. "First of all—her family up and left town out of nowhere."

"That's not super weird, is it? People move."

"Yeah but she built this big-ass mansion right outside of town for them to live in. Or, they started building it, and then suddenly they stopped building it, and then suddenly her family's old house was for sale, and they were gone."

"Should I be taking notes?" August said.

"Careful, that's like foreplay to Sophie," Brit replied, and I rolled my eyes. "So she abandons the house. Her family leaves town. Then her third album comes out, and the lead single—the biggest song off it—is all about leaving home and never going back."

August frowned. "So? Songs can be fictional."

"Soooo, naturally everyone asked her about it in interviews, like, 'Hey, Megan, didn't you write that one song about how your hometown is great? Tell us more about how you've followed it up with one that says you want to burn it to the ground.'"

"What'd she say?"

"That the message in the song is pretty clear."

"What's the message?"

"You heard the 'burn it to the ground' part, right?" Brit said.

"Why does she hate it, though?"

"No one knows."

"Hm." August glanced up at the ceiling, a little wrinkle between his brows. For a few moments, there was just the *thwack* of the Ping-Pong paddles and the hollow sound of the ball hitting the table. "Could be worth investigating," he said finally, glancing over at me. "Don't you think?"

"Why?"

"Figuring out why she doesn't want to come back here . . . *if* that's the case"—he added, when he saw my expression—"seems important to getting her back here." A pause. "It's like . . . the last prong. Of the multipronged approach. Right?"

I had the sudden urge to grab both sides of his face and kiss him soundly.

Instead, I just nodded.

"Right."


That night I took out my planning notebook and added a category to the Megan Pleasant fall festival page:

*Social Media Outreach*

*Local Contacts*

*State Fair*

I wrote the word *INVESTIGATION* in big letters and under-lined it twice.

# eighteen

I began my research that night, starting with a profile of Megan from a while back titled A PLEASANT PLACE: THIRD ALBUM SEES COUNTRY DARLING IN A NEW STATE OF MIND.

*At twenty-two, country star Megan Pleasant is poised to release her third studio album,* Foundation. *The follow-up to her sophomore album,* Letters Home, Foundation *is a departure for the breakout second runner-up of the first season of* America's Next Country Star. *I sat down with Pleasant at a café in Nashville to discuss her career, her upcoming album, and a potential homecoming—or lack thereof.*

*"It's been a wild ride," she says of her journey from reality-show hopeful to certified-gold country star. "There have been moments*

along the way where it almost didn't feel real. Like it's all something that was happening to someone else. But it's a dream come true. I've always wanted to sing country. There was never any doubt. That's where my heart is."

While some of Pleasant's contemporaries have viewed country as a stepping-stone to more widespread commercial success in the pop genre, Pleasant has carefully skirted a full-on transition into pop. "No one would mistake these songs for anything but country," Pleasant's producer, John Humes, has said of Foundation. "Megan's a hometown girl. She's authentic. I think she's drawn not only to the country sound, but to the kind of vibe that comes with it, where what you see is what you get."

With Pleasant's reality-show roots—was there ever a feeling of having to prove herself within the industry, of having to work twice as hard to be taken seriously? Pleasant shakes her head quickly. "It's not a competition," she says with a wry smile. "At least, not anymore."

Pleasant dreamed of stardom from a young age, singing in talent shows and the church choir in her rural town of Acadia, Illinois, which she immortalized in her first breakout hit, the hometown tribute of "Gave You My Heartland." "Heartland" was a salute to Pleasant's small-town roots, a theme that is woven throughout her first and second albums.

The juxtaposition with "Steel Highway," the lead single from Foundation, is stark. With lyrics like "burn it down / salt the earth / you'll never see my face again," and "Lord help me, I'm never going back," "Steel Highway" is perhaps Pleasant's darkest track to date, a far cry both lyrically and musically from the sweet simplicity of her previous albums. Pleasant's self-titled debut features odes to "morning glories and summer nights," "true love's kiss," and "love on the wind." "Steel Highway" represents a clear departure.

The question on everyone's mind: Is the place that put the "heart" in "Heartland" the very same subject of Foundation's scorched-earth anthem? Is the girl who penned a towering salute to her hometown now a woman vowing never to return?

"You could interpret it that way," she says. "Although in this case, there's not much to interpret. It's pretty specific."

I refer to an interview with MTV from several years prior, in which Pleasant spoke of hoping to one day raise a family in Acadia. Her response?

"Everyone thinks things when they're young that end up being untrue, don't they? Here's a great scoop: your favorite singers might too."

We are into our second beverages when Pleasant turns the questions on me—what did I want to be when I was younger? Did I always want to live in Los Angeles? Did I ever think I would write for a magazine? And the question that makes her eyes light up over her coffee mug—when did I experience first love? (Tenth grade, for the record.)

"You felt like you would love them forever, right? Like they were the be-all and end-all of your entire existence? She—were they a she? She was probably the light of your life, wasn't she? And what does she do now?" I hadn't seen her in years, and I say as much. "If you could get in a time machine and go back to high school and tell yourself that there would be a day on this earth when you didn't know where she was, or what she was doing—what made her smile, what broke her heart, how she did her hair, what perfume she wore— if you told yourself that, you would never have believed it. Right? But everyone changes. The way you feel about people changes. Same goes for places, I guess."

We have steered back to "Steel Highway," and I hate to break the quiet calm, but I have to press on—what caused the rift with Acadia?

Pleasant just smiles and takes a sip of her drink. Almond milk steamer, two pumps of vanilla. Her eyes shine. "What was her name?"

# nineteen

We decided to start our official investigation on Saturday with a trip to Megan's mansion. Brit was free, and bored, so I told her we'd swing by her place on our way out there.

First I went over to Kyle and Heather's to collect August.

Heather's car was in the driveway, so I crossed around to the back door. Shepherd barked like crazy whenever anyone came to the front.

As I approached, I could hear voices wafting out the screen door—Heather saying, "No. For real. It's not necessary."

"It's fine," August replied gruffly. "I don't mind pitching in."

"I don't want you to feel like you have to earn your keep here, though."

"I don't feel like that. And it doesn't have to be . . . weird or whatever. Whenever I get paid, I'll just leave it here. In . . . the most horrifying cookie jar on earth—"

"Creepy Cookie," Heather said. "Cady was terrified of it when she was a toddler, that's why we had to keep it up there."

"You could've kept it in the garbage. Or . . . sent it back to the depths of hell."

Heather snorted. "It was a present from Kyle's grandma. But yeah, I agree."

A pause. "I'll just put it in Creepy Cookie," August said. "We never have to talk about it."

Another pause, and when Heather responded finally, she sounded resigned: "Not everything, though. Keep at least half. At *least*. For . . . going out with your friends, or . . . saving for school."

"Yeah, okay," August replied, and then it was quiet again.

When I tapped on the door and stuck my head in, August was alone, stuffing a roll of cash into the hideous cookie jar that sat atop the fridge. I was fairly certain it was the money Heather had just told him to keep, the *at least half* he had agreed to. He turned, and for a brief moment a complicated series of emotions flashed across his face before settling into something neutral.

"Ready to go?" I said.

He turned back to Creepy Cookie, which was a gray clay jar fashioned into a weird humanlike shape with a large bulging stomach and small hands and feet sticking out of it. The top of the jar was Creepy Cookie's head, which August moved back onto its neck.

"Let's do it," he replied, but then paused, considering Creepy Cookie. He reached up again and turned the head so that the face was pointed toward the wall. "Better or worse?"

"Honestly? I think it's a toss-up."

"It's just past those trees up there," I told August as we neared the site of Megan's would-be house, having retrieved Brit and biked over.

"The Pleasant place," Brit said with relish.

August waggled his eyebrows. "I know a thing or two about a pleasant place."

"Save it," Brit replied. "No one wants your clarinet dick."

The mansion was a little ways out of town and set back from the road, off a drive that wound through a bit of woods.

It was actually two houses—or the remains of an old house with the shell of a new one attached to the back of it. The original part was an old farmhouse that supposedly Megan had wanted to restore. A giant addition was tacked on the back, but neither part of the renovation was ever completed.

There had been talk of the town buying it and turning it into some kind of a museum—the Acadia Historical Society brought it up—but I don't think they had the funds for that. So it sat vacant, the grass growing tall around it.

We dropped our bikes by the front and stared up at the house.

"What are we waiting for?" Brit said, and started forward.

I grabbed her arm. "What are you doing?"

"We didn't ride all the way out here just to look at it. We're going in, aren't we?" And she strode up to the front of the house.

Brit reached the door by the time I caught up, climbing the steps to the wide front porch, which was another add-on to the original structure. The porch was just bare wood, unpainted and badly weathered. It would've been lovely if it were finished—a cushioned porch swing swaying in the breeze. Condensation on a pitcher of lemonade. That kind of thing.

Brit turned the handle on the front door. It was locked, but the door gave a bit against the pressure.

She rattled it a few times. "We could probably knock it open." She looked back at August. "Wanna give it a whirl?"

He shook his head. "I'm not trying to make this into a genuine breaking-and-entering situation."

"But we're not going to learn anything new by just standing out here!"

"You don't even care about the whole Megan thing anyway," I said.

"I care deeply about doing something interesting," Brit replied, and went back down to retrieve August, urging him up the steps from behind. "Come on, August ol' boy, give that door a good shoulder. Show us all the . . . raw power in that . . . tight . . . body of yours"— she sputtered a laugh—"I'm sorry, I can't even pretend like that's true—"

"If you care so much, you do the breaking in," August said.

"I can't risk it. I have to stay in top physical form."

"Maybe I do too."

"To do what? Shill sponges at Dollar Depot? Get to punching down that door."

August was about to speak when I held up a hand. "There's a way in. It's in the back."

"Awesome," August said, at the same time Brit said, "How do you know that?"

I had heard people talking about it at school—this was briefly a party spot, before the cops started routinely buzzing by on weekend nights. "I know it's shocking, but I occasionally know stuff."

"But illicit stuff, though?" Brit said.

"It's not *illicit*."

"You were the one who said we shouldn't go in."

I sighed. "We're just . . . briefly surveying. For research. We'll be fine."

"You're the one who's gonna tell the cops it's for research, okay?" August said, following me around back. "I really feel like they'll believe you."

"Why?"

"You have an honest face."

"I could be a huge liar, you wouldn't know."

"Tell me a lie right now."

I picked my way through the tall grass. "When I was seven, I entered the firehouse's annual hot-dog-eating contest. I ate half a hot dog and then threw up, and then cried a lot, and they made me honorary winner because they felt bad for me."

He looked at me for a moment. "It's true. You're trying to trick me."

I grinned. "It's a lie. I knew you'd think I was going to do that."

I would never tell him he was right.

We reached the particular spot in the back, and just as the girls from school had said, there was a wooden board covering a large window that was attached loosely enough at the top that you could push it to the side and slip through. We did just that.

It was dim inside. This part of the house was basically a shell— unfinished floors, drywall only.

I could tell it would be a nice place if it was ever finished. The kitchen was giant—an island outlined on the floor, chalk marks laid down for where the appliances would go. A long hallway branched off to the right, a large doorway straight ahead opened up into the old side of the house, where a staircase led up to the second floor.

We didn't venture upstairs, just poked around a bit on the first floor, not saying much to each other. There was nothing with which to really draw a conclusion about Megan or her departure, besides the unfinished nature of everything that spoke of said departure.

When we headed outside again, we sat down by our bikes, looking up at the place. "It is interesting, though," August said eventually. "That addition is huge. Why would you start something like that and then abandon it?"

It was quiet.

"Maybe she witnessed a murder," Brit murmured.

"Brit!"

"We're spitballing!" she said. "There's no harm in spitballing!"

August grinned. "Does she have a song about murder? Or one that implies having witnessed a murder?"

Brit's eyes widened. "She does actually."

"Really?"

"Yeah. 'Murder Creek Murder: The Knife Is Behind That Rock.'"

"Okay, you were the one who suggested murder—"

"There's a follow-up single too," I said. "It's called 'Remember the Time There Was That Murder? I Do, and It Haunts Me.'"

"By Megan Pleasant," Brit continued. "All rights reserved. People and events represented are entirely fictional, except for the murder—that part's real."

"Why do I even—Why do you—" August sputtered, but he was fighting a laugh.

Brit laughed mercilessly, and I couldn't help but join in.

Brit parted ways with us on the ride back. It was quiet as August and I dismounted our bikes outside the Conlins' house.

"So she wrote a song about Acadia," he said, like he had been contemplating it this whole time. "About loving Acadia."

I nodded. "'Gave You My Heartland.' A different thing to do in Acadia for every day of the week. It was her first big hit."

"We should probably do it, don't you think?"

Something in my brain short-circuited. "Sorry?"

"The Megan Pleasant week. Let's do it. Everything in the song."

August was proposing we do the "Gave You My Heartland" week. A song that was ostensibly about different locations throughout Acadia, but was also very much about falling in love with someone over the course of a week at said locations. Did he know that? Was he—did this mean—

"Why?" was all I could say.

He looked away, shifting his weight from one foot to the other.

"For research or whatever," he said. "To properly inhabit her mind-set."

I blinked.

"And to get to know the town," he continued. "It'll be multipronged." And he glanced back with a smile that I couldn't help but return. "Let's go bowling on Monday and do the hokey pokey on Tuesday and whatever the hell else she says we should do."

He didn't know, then. About the falling in love part. "Hokey pokey isn't one of the things."

"You know what I mean. Line-dancing on Wednesdays. Pulling a rusty bucket out of a well on Thursday."

"I'm going to poke you."

"Tip a cow on Friday. Fuck a bale of hay on Saturday."

It was hard not to laugh, but I just leveled him with a stare. He grinned, almost sheepish but not quite.

"Okay. I'll stop."

I drew the silence out until he looked away, smile faltering with something close to an apology.

"If you listened to the song," I said finally, "you'd know we fuck bales of hay on Thursdays."

He grinned.

# twenty

On Monday, we went to Miller's—*Monday nights at Miller's, pitchers for five and a booth for two.*

We both ordered chicken tenders and fries. We couldn't get pitchers for five, not only because we weren't old enough to order them, but because Miller's raised the price of their Monday-night pitchers following the fame of "Gave You My Heartland."

After we ordered, August looked at me, drumming his fingers against the table. "So after we do this—like once we finish the whole week, is the ritual complete? Do we have to cut our palms and dance around a fire and then Megan Pleasant will appear and grant us three wishes?"

"I guess there is something kind of . . . ritualistic about it. They used to do tours and stuff."

"For real?"

"Uh-huh. All the spots—here, Tropicana, the bridge, everything."

"Isn't one of them out in the middle of a field?"

I raised an eyebrow. "So you listened to it."

He began opening packs of sugar and dumping them into his iced tea. "Of course I listened. Do you think I'd go into this unprepared? What if there's something crazy in there, like lassoing a bull, or jumping off a building?"

"Then we'd be lassoing and jumping for the full Megan Pleasant experience."

"Here's to that," August said, lifting his cup. I knocked mine against it.

On Tuesday, we went to the lake—*skipping stones, watching clouds go by*.

The lake was not truly a lake. Acadia had a few ponds—one back by the Pritchetts' farm, one near the highway with a little creek running into it. A dip in one of the fields by school filled up sometimes when it rained, but we figured that Megan wasn't referring to that one. Context clues in the song led everyone to believe it was the pond that August and I were currently standing in front of—the one in Fairview Park, ringed by willows.

We tried to skip stones. August had never done it before. I managed to get three skips, and he crowed when he got two.

"Did you see that?"

"Not bad."

"Not bad? That was expert level!"

"If you're expert level, then what am I?"

"God level." He tried again, and the rock sank with a *thunk*, sending up a small spray of water. "I'd build a monument to you, but I'm fresh out of rocks."

Wednesday was for ice cream cones, after we both finished at work.

"Technically we've already done this one," August said, and took a swipe at his mint-chocolate-chip cone.

"Yeah, well, technically, we should be alone," I replied, looking pointedly at Terrance.

August's eyes shone. "Sophie's right. The song doesn't mention a third wheel."

"It doesn't say there *isn't* one either," Terrance said with a grin.

"Schrödinger's lyric," August said. "There both is and isn't a third wheel until Megan confirms."

"There's definitely a third wheel," I said. "I can confirm it right now."

We went downtown on Thursday.

We were supposed to *drift from one shop to the next, shooting the breeze.* A number of shops lined the street downtown—the weird old antique shop; the hardware store; Mrs. Weaver's bakery. Every small town I'd been to seemed to have something super random too, like a coin shop, or a pipe-organ store. In our case, it was a vacuum-cleaner-repair shop that was never open but somehow never went out of business. Maybe they serviced one vacuum cleaner a year and lived on that lone repair.

I told August this, and he nodded in consideration. "Could be possible."

"Fifty grand to fix your vacuum."

"I mean, that's a deal. My vacuum cost twelve million dollars."

"Really."

"Uh-huh. Military-grade. It could drain a lake."

I grinned. "If you aim it at the sky, it's capable of tearing a hole in the fabric of space."

We headed to the antique store after stopping by the Yum Yum Shoppe to try some fudge and say hi to Terrance. Thankfully, he didn't decide to take his break and tag along.

The antique store was called Bygones. It was small but crammed with stuff divided up into little booths. Nothing really of value, to be honest, unless you were interested in old embroidered dish towels and McDonald's toys from the early nineties. Our neighbor across the street, Mrs. Cabot, had a booth there; she'd trawl through town on garbage day, picking out any furniture she could find. She'd fix the stuff up and paint it and try to resell it. I was in there once with Brit and her mom when Brit's mom recognized a chair she had put out for the trash a few weeks previous.

*She's charging twenty-seven dollars! For my garbage! TWENTY-SEVEN-DOLLAR GARBAGE.*

Today we paused at a booth with shelves lining each side. I investigated one crammed full of paperbacks with broken spines. When I glanced over at August, he was looking at an old red-white-and-blue trophy, a little gold plastic football player stuck on top of it.

"You know, Kyle played football," I said.

"Not surprising," he replied, and then it was quiet, except for the whir of the floor fan at the end of the aisle.

"Have you guys gotten to do any . . . brother-bonding stuff?"

"Like what?"

"I don't know. I don't have a brother."

"Half brother," he murmured, and put the trophy back.

"You say that like it means something." Some particular kind of line that needed to be drawn. "Like he's fifty percent less your brother."

"It means exactly that he's fifty percent my brother."

"Well, yeah, genetically." I thought of Ciara, her freshman-year biology course and the Punnett squares that could predict what color eyes her and Ravi's kids would have. "But where it counts . . . it means nothing. You know, my sister, Ciara"—a pause—"my mom and her dad got married when I was a baby. Her dad—our dad—adopted me."

"So you're not actually related?"

136

"By your standards, she is exactly zero percent my sister. But by everything that counts . . . she's—she—"

In second grade I remember a girl in my class—Lizzie Bowen—standing on the playground at lunch and telling me that Ciara couldn't possibly be my sister.

"You don't look like each other," she said. "You have to look alike. Me and my sisters do. Dash and Terrance do."

I looked over at Dash and Terrance, who were playing four-square with Brit and Flora. They did have the same deep brown skin, the same brown eyes. But it was more than that—Dash was bigger, Terrance was small and skinny, but their faces were definitely similar. Two different takes on the same idea.

"You and her don't look like each other," Lizzie insisted. "So you're not real sisters."

"We are!"

"Not *real* ones. You have to say *step*. She's your *step*sister."

I shook my head vehemently. I knew at that point that our family was built differently than other people's—the events had happened out of order but put us together the same way, which was what counted the most. Ciara was my sister. I knew that at my core.

I told her as we walked home that day, trying to keep the tremble out of my voice, eyes turned down to the ground as we made our way through our neighborhood.

"She doesn't know what she's talking about," Ciara replied.

"But—"

"She's wrong," she said firmly, and I believed her.

When I finally looked over at August, in the booth at Bygones, there was a softness to his expression that I wasn't prepared for. I turned back to the books, pulled one out at random. It was a paperback called *Summer Burn*, with a man and a woman silhouetted on the cover, their foreheads touching.

I ended up getting the book, after we had passed through the remaining booths, since I felt bad coming in without buying anything. Supporting local business and all that. It put me out two dollars, which I could manage, if Brit sponsored her own french fries this week.

I read August part of the description as we stood at the front, waiting for the cashier. "'Will Declan escape unscathed, or will Summer consume him?'"

"You'll have to let me know," August said.

"Oh, Summer is ten out of ten gonna consume him. But I'll keep you posted."

The cashier emerged from one of the aisles, an older lady.

"You should've rung the bell!" she said brightly, heading behind the counter. She smiled at me and then looked at August.

"Back already?"

He looked sheepish. "Yeah, just . . . having a look."

"That's how you find the deals. You gotta keep coming back around. The inventory's always changing!"

She rang up my book, and we headed outside.

"You've been there before?"

"Maybe," he said, and looked embarrassed. "I just . . . was trying to sell some leftover stuff. From back home. Just"—he shrugged—"make some extra money or whatever."

I thought about the money in Creepy Cookie and wondered if he was thinking about it too.

We headed down Main Street. "My mom used to take me and my sister to garage sales all the time when we were kids," I said after a pause. "Like on Saturday mornings and stuff, we'd drive for miles to find a good sale. Ciara called it 'treasure hunting.' It always felt like an adventure."

"Do you still go?"

I nodded. "Sometimes."

It was quiet for a moment. "That place felt kind of like treasure hunting," he said, gesturing back to Bygones.

He was right—it did.

On Friday, we went bowling.

"I have to warn you, I'm an incredible bowler," August said. "Like, truly, staggeringly talented."

He bowled an impressive five gutter balls in a row.

"Is that what you mean by staggeringly talented?"

He grinned. "Yeah. I'm the best worst bowler in the world. Try to find a worse bowler than me."

According to the song, on Saturday we were meant to go to the covered bridge and tell each other things we've never said out loud before: *what's in my heart, and yours . . .*

So we went and stood on the bridge, looking out at the creek below, which was really more of a ditch, all dried out in the summer heat.

"So," August said. "What are we supposed to do?"

I recited the lyric for him.

"Is it two separate things?" he mused. "Stuff we've never said out loud *and* stuff that's in our heart, or stuff in our hearts that we've never said out loud?"

"Mmm . . . up to interpretation, I guess?"

"Okay, alternate third interpretation, stuff that we've never said out loud that happens to be in *both* of our hearts?" He blinked. "How am I supposed to know what's in your heart?"

"We're each speaking for our own hearts, I think."

"She should've been more clear. Lyrically."

"Do you want to keep analyzing this, or do you want to do what the song says?"

"Hey, this song is your bible, not mine."

"It's not my *bible.*"

"It's your town's bible."

"Are we going to do this or not?"

"Okay." He took a deep breath. "Okay. Ummmm . . ." Silence. "Maybe you go first."

I paused. Something in my heart that I've never said out loud before.

I thought of band and work and the library. I thought of *The College Collective.*

"I don't want to go away," I said. "For school. Like . . . part of me wishes I could just stay here forever. But . . . if I know it'll make me a better person, then I'll leave. And I feel like it will. Or, like, I hope it will, at least."

"Why do you want to be a better person? You're already—" He shook his head. "You're good."

I shrugged. "Everyone can be better."

His eyes were suddenly serious. "Do you really think that?"

"Sure." I leaned against the railing, peering down into the ditch below. "Your turn."

August was quiet for a moment, until: "I hate bacon."

I looked back over at him.

"People put it in everything, and it sucks."

"Are you kidding me?"

"What?"

"We are speaking *from the heart*, August."

"My heart hates bacon. And in the long run, it's probably a good choice. My heart is smart."

"I told you—I just—You were the one who said you wanted to do this whole thing for real, you said—"

I pivoted away, ready to leave, but August grabbed my arm.

"Okay. All right. Sorry."

I turned to look at him.

"But the bacon thing is real, and I've never said that out loud." A pause. "Okay. I . . . ." He sighed. "I, um. I like staying with Kyle and Heather. And the girls."

"That's it?"

"I haven't said it out loud. But it's . . . in my . . . whatever."

"But that's not even like . . . That's normal. You should like living with them, and you should say it out loud. To them."

"What did you want? Some deep, dark secret?"

"No, geez. Just . . . something . . ." More vulnerable. "I don't know. Whatever. Never mind."

"Sometimes I miss them," he said.

"Like . . . when they're not home?"

"Like when they're sitting next to me. When we're watching TV or doing something random."

"Why?"

He shook his head, and I didn't know if it meant he didn't know or that he didn't want to say.

Late Sunday afternoon found August and me on our very last "Gave You My Heartland" mission in a field tucked away behind school.

We spread a blanket out on the grass and lay down. Enough space stretched between us to satisfy my Sunday school teacher, though I don't know how thrilled she'd be about the whole situation in general.

Then again, I went to school with her kids, and if rumors served, I knew they had done way saucier stuff than lying on blankets in an effort to re-create "Gave You My Heartland."

I glanced over at August, and I couldn't help but think of what he had said at Miller's on Monday—*Of course I listened. Do you think I'd go into this unprepared?*

That meant that he must've known what was coming. He wasn't entirely unaware of the final verse: *Out in the field on the blanket, your lips on mine* . . .

"So," August said. "What now?"

"Well." I spoke carefully. "We're supposed to kiss. I guess. Technically."

He looked over at me. "What do you think?"

"What do you mean, what do I think?"

"Should we?"

"Should we?" I repeated. Was he serious?

"For research," he said. "Or authenticity, or whatever."

"I . . ." I took a moment. Really looked at him. A hint of a smirk played around his lips, and amusement flashed in his eyes, which were very warm and very bright from this distance. If Flora were in my place, she'd probably write a poem about something like the *kaleidoscope of colors* in those eyes, and Brit would probably make fun of her for it.

There was something else in his eyes too, something I couldn't describe any better than I could the *kaleidoscope of colors*. August seemed nothing if not self-assured, but he looked away after a pause, his Adam's apple bobbing on a swallow, and maybe I doubted it for just a moment.

"Yeah, okay," I said.

This was a bad idea, and I knew it. Like Brit trying to dip-dye my hair in seventh grade. But it was borne of wanting. I wanted pink hair. I wanted August.

He smiled and moved closer, but paused at the last moment, very close.

"Just for research, okay?" he murmured, voice uncharacteristically serious.

A bad idea for sure.

I nodded anyway.

# twenty-one

I have no idea how long August and I made out. If you told me seasons had changed, a dozen Super Bowls had come and gone, society was now on the iPhone 54X—I'd believe it. Because it was impossible to mark time, to gauge it, to even care, with August's mouth on mine, my hands in his hair.

This was not how I saw this going. But I wasn't complaining.

Eventually, August's phone rang.

I pulled away. "Should you get it?"

"No." Kiss. Kiss. "Phones don't exist here."

"It could be something important."

"Nope."

The ringing stopped. We kept kissing, for another few minutes, or through the rise and fall of the digital age.

Then it rang again.

"August."

He made a noise equivalent to *SFDLKJDFSKHJ* and sat up, pulling his phone from his back pocket. I could see HEATHER flashing across the screen.

"Hello?"

A pause. I touched my fingers to my lips.

"Yeah, okay . . . Yes . . . I don't know, what time is it? . . . Okay. Yeah, soon . . ." His eyes widened suddenly. "No, no, no. Here, talk to Sophie—" He flung the phone at me.

I managed to grab it and sat up too. "Hello?"

"Sophie?"

"Yeah."

"I didn't know you guys were together."

Something in my chest seized. "We're not. We're just friends."

A pause. "I meant, like, hanging out right now."

"Oh. Oh yeah."

"Well, anyway, Cady wanted to talk to August but I guess he's busy?"

August had gotten up from the blanket and walked away, stopping a few yards off with his back to me. The way his shirt hugged his shoulders was . . . not terrible.

"Yeah, sorry."

"Okay, well, let him know she expects him for dinner. It's pizza night. Last time he did this thing where he ordered in a funny voice? She thinks it's, like, the absolute height of prank comedy."

146

"I'll tell him."

"Hey, and while you're here, can you do Tuesday at five instead of six?"

"Yeah, no problem."

"Awesome. Thanks, Soph!" She hung up.

I set the phone aside. August turned back, his face chagrined.

"What was that?" I said as he approached the blanket again. He flopped back down but facing me now, leaning back on his hands.

"I couldn't talk to Cady! After we were just . . . when we were all . . . worked up."

"Worked up? You were worked up?"

"Actually, no. Never mind. I felt nothing."

I grinned.

He grinned back. "So. Did we do Megan Pleasant justice?"

My smile dimmed a little. It was over. We weren't going to go back to making out. This exercise, this adventure, whatever it was, was finished.

I nodded. "Yeah. She'd be super proud."

"Good." He bobbed his head. "Good, yeah."

"What do you think, having done the whole thing now?"

"I think I have a new appreciation for it?" He wrinkled his nose. "Or at least for Acadia."

"So you love it now?"

"Maybe not full-on love. Maybe just like *L-O*."

"You're halfway there," I said.

So was I.

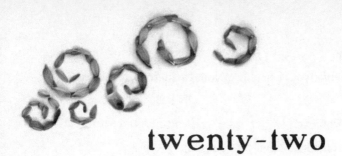

# twenty-two

Flora brought home food from work that night, and we sat outside at the patio table in her backyard to eat. She still had on her uniform, and smelled like french fry grease, but she chatted easily anyway, like she hadn't just been standing for eight hours, like she wasn't exhausted from dealing with free refills and mixed-up orders and the general public. Further validating Brit's argument that Flora might just operate on an elevated plane of existence.

I knew she got cranky sometimes, like anyone else. She missed her dad when he was away. She'd get annoyed with Brit over little things. But she was one of those people, my mom would say, who have a light inside of them that you can't help but be drawn to. The kind of person who makes other people feel warm. When Flora looked at you, you felt like she saw the best version of you. Or at least, she made you want to be that version.

Tonight, she said "firefly" whenever we saw one, which was pretty often on a summer evening. We had been talking a bit about something on TV last night ("I don't think he'll survive elimination, but if he did—firefly—I wouldn't be mad") until Flora said, "Let's make-believe."

I stared up at the sky. Make-believe was Flora's favorite—it's when we talked about Other Acadia, and our fabulous lives there.

"You've just gotten back from the mall," I said. Other Acadia had a luxury mall, of course. "You bought a super expensive purse, and you picked up exactly what you wanted for dinner—"

"Chicken nuggets," she supplied, mouth full.

"Perfect. You've picked up the chicken nuggets, you drive home in your fancy car, and eat dinner—"

"Outside, with you."

"You know, Other Acadia isn't that different from regular Acadia tonight."

"We're next to a pool, though."

"Cool. Are we wearing caftans?"

"Oh yeah. Designer caftans," she said, and licked some sauce off her fingers. "What have you been doing all day in Other Acadia?"

"Just hanging out."

"With August?"

"Sure." My voice stayed so even, I surprised myself: "Other Acadia August actually likes me back."

I didn't shift my gaze away from the treetops, but I didn't need to. I could feel Flora's eyes on me.

"Actual Acadia August likes you, though."

I shook my head. "Not like that. Not like how I do."

"He does."

I paused. "How do you know that?"

It wasn't unthinkable that someone had seen us out in the field today. Maybe Flora knew we kissed. Maybe she thought that was proof enough, but I knew the truth—Brit kissed enough people for me to know that you could do so without it meaning anything. Just because it's fun, or you're bored, or you felt like it.

Flora shrugged. "I just do."

I didn't want to talk about it anymore, even though I was the one who brought it up. Flora had a way of drawing stuff out of you, stuff you weren't sure you were ready to confront yourself.

"Have you been doing your social media outreach?" I said instead.

Flora made a face. "Let's just enjoy summer."

"You sound like Brit."

I thought she was going to say something more about it, but she threw her head back and looked at the sky.

"Firefly," she said instead.

# twenty-three

Band rehearsals started back up the next week in preparation for the Fourth of July parade. We would be marching with our program for the Rose Parade, as well as a few other standards—the fight song, some current pop hits.

Our Rose Parade show theme was "Sounds of the '60s." It was a medley of three songs: "Windy" by the Association, "Build Me Up Buttercup" by the Foundations, and "Reach Out I'll Be There" by the Four Tops.

"Windy" was happy and bouncy and fun and kind of meaningless. Like, as a song, the lyrics were definitely absurd, but the music was undeniably feel-good. "Build Me Up Buttercup" was a deceptive song in that it sounded incredibly bouncy and fun, and, barring the lyrics, it was, but the lyrics themselves were pretty depressing. Luckily we were just extracting the instrumentals.

"Reach Out" was my favorite—the band arrangement was incredible. The drums, the brass, everything built into a giant wall of sound over the course of the song. It was perfect to march to.

The first day back in rehearsal, I took my seat in the woodwinds section. Two girls from my class, Chelsea and Becca, were sitting in front of me, fussing with their instruments.

"I was there on Saturday, but I didn't see him."

"Jess said he usually works mornings. Sophie probably knows." Chelsea suddenly turned around to me.

"Sorry?"

"The new guy."

"The *hot* new guy," Becca clarified.

"As opposed to the not-hot new guy? There is only one new guy. He is hot, and you know him," Chelsea said.

"Is he single?" Becca added, before I could answer.

"Uh . . . yeah, I think?"

"You guys aren't a thing? Someone said they saw you at Miller's last week."

"We were just . . ." *Doing "Gave You My Heartland"?* That wouldn't fly. I shrugged, and it came out so much more casually than it felt: "We're just friends."

"Awesome," Chelsea said, and they both turned away.

It sounded foolish, but I hadn't really thought about what it would be like having August in school with us. Meeting people at parties was one thing, but when school started, we would have to share him for real. What if he found people he liked better?

*We*, I told myself. This was definitely my concerns for we, the group, and not me, the person who had spent several nights staring at the ceiling and thinking of the feeling of August's lips on mine.

I threw myself into rehearsal.

I genuinely liked being back in the swing of it, even if we were just in the band room to start, running through our program. First we needed to get the music going all together. Then we needed a balance to the performance—the brass could easily overwhelm, like a soprano who sang too loud. The drum line needed to be crisp and precise.

Ms. Hill gave us instructions, and we broke things down and put them together again, and it felt good to be back.


We reconvened at Teen Zone 2 after rehearsal.

I stopped at home to drop off my clarinet and hung around waiting for Flora, but she texted me saying to go on ahead. When I arrived, everyone else was there, including August, who was settling on the couch as Brit fussed with the laptop set up on the Ping-Pong table.

"We're watching a movie," she announced. "I already picked for us."

"How gracious of you," I said.

"I do what I can."

We had just settled in and started the movie when everyone's phones buzzed. A message from Flora:

*Sorry, still held up at home, be there soon!!!*

"What is it?" August said.

"Flora's on her way," I replied. We were a few minutes back into the film when I said, "We should add you to the group chat. Then you'll get everyone's messages too."

Brit raised her eyebrows. "You want to add him to WWYSE?"

"Why not?" I could hear her voice at the party some weeks back: *So we're officially adopting him now?*

"WWYSE is a commitment," Brit said. "It's forever."

"Forever?" August repeated.

"It's just a group chat," I said.

"Excuse me, it is not *just* a group chat. When someone asks where you'll spend eternity, you are contractually obligated to respond."

"Is there paperwork?" August asked.

"Soph, I love you, but we're not adding some . . . passing crush to the group," Brit said.

"He's not—you're not—" I squeezed my eyes shut briefly, breathed through my nose.

"Rage headache?" Terrance's voice.

"Brit headache."

"Same thing."

Three phones dinged.

I checked mine—a message from Brit.

*If he's in the chat, we can't talk about your M A J O R B O N E R for him.*

"Brit. Come on."

"Say it in the chat, that's what it's there for," she replied.

*I hate you.*

*OPPOSITES*, she replied, followed by a string of hearts.

We went into the house for snacks later, but Brit and August stayed outside, lingering on the back patio.

I could hear them through the screen door as Terrance poked through the fridge and Dash investigated the cabinets. Terrance and Dash had their own kind of shorthand established:

"There should be more—"

"Uh-huh. Do you want—"

"You know it."

So I was free to listen in on Brit and August.

"You get it about the chat, right?" Brit was saying. They had settled on the steps outside the back door, facing out into the yard. "It's more than just jokes, you know. It's like . . . our friend-group thing. Not that you're—it's nothing personal, I'm just saying. We've known each other for . . . our whole lives, basically. Compared to that, you're a blip. We've been friends for long before you got here, and we'll be friends long after, you know?"

That was harsh as hell, wasn't it? I wanted to keep August with us, not lose him to some other friend group, to Chelsea and Becca from band or whoever.

I almost pushed through the door until I heard August speak.

"I get it. Just . . . seemed important to Sophie."

"Everything's important to Sophie. She cries when people get voted off reality shows." She shook her head. "But she would never let you see her crying when someone gets voted off a reality show, because then you might feel sad or uncomfortable, and she doesn't want anyone to feel anything less than happy all the time. She's . . . the strongest person I've ever known."

August paused. "Is that a joke?"

"What about her would make you think that was a joke?"

"Not Sophie, you. You just . . . usually make jokes."

"I can take shit seriously," she said. "I would jump off a bridge if she asked me to. Because I know she wouldn't ask without a really good reason."

August was quiet. *Where's the joke?* I wondered, because the same could be said for him.

"She's a thousand times better than both of us," Brit said. "So just . . . keep that in mind, okay?"

I didn't understand Brit. She was the one saying she'd *wingman the shit out of this* for me. I didn't get how this fit in.

I pushed through the door.

Brit glanced back at me, then stood. "You guys need snack supervision? I want melted cheese on everything."

"Better get on that, then," I said.

So she went back in, and I sat down next to August.

We hadn't hung out alone together since the last day of "Gave You My Heartland" week. The kiss day.

It was only weird if we made it weird. Right?

I was thinking about what to say to convey that it wasn't weird when August spoke:

"So, uh, I asked Kyle. About Megan. For the whole . . . investigation thing."

"Oh." Megan was, for once, nowhere near the forefront of my mind. "Cool. What'd he say?"

"She was a year behind him in school. He said he knew her a little, but she was out of town a lot when she was on the TV show, and after it ended, she wasn't around much. I don't think she actually graduated."

Her first album came out when she was sixteen. It made sense she wouldn't have a lot of time for school.

"Does he know anyone who kept in touch with her?"

August shook his head. "No. Sorry."

"Heather know anything?"

"She said they had gym together, and Megan was, quote, *terrible at everything involving balls*."

I let out a breath of laughter. "I'll make a note of that."

And just like that, it wasn't weird.

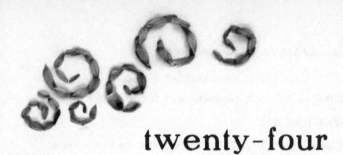

# twenty-four

The Fourth of July parade was one of my favorite things in Acadia.

It always had an abstract theme, like "Let the Good Times Roll" or "A Town of Neighbors and Friends," that seemed nearly impossible to translate into an actual float. The businesses and churches in town would do their best, decorating pickup trucks or pulling a flatbed covered in crepe paper and poster board, pinwheels and banners.

The scouts decorated their bikes and rode together in a pack. The sports teams from school and the cheerleaders would ride in the back of trucks or walk alongside. The Yum Yum Shoppe would go up and down the street pulling coolers filled with cups of ice cream for sale.

The band marched, of course. It was too hot at midday for full uniforms, so we wore khaki shorts and our blue Marching Pride of Acadia T-shirts. We lined up in the parking lot at school and joined the queue of floats heading to Main Street.

As we marched, I passed my parents seated with Flora's mom and grandma. A little farther down were the Conlins. Heather had Harper on her lap, and Cadence stood next to August, who was sitting on the curb. Cadence was clutching a bag to collect candy that people threw from the floats.

They both waved as we went by. The drum line took over at just the right time, so I had a hand free to wave back.

The band worked the barbecue, in association with the Lions Club. Mainly we bussed tables, but a portion of the profits would go toward fundraising, so it was worth it. That's what I told myself as I cleared trash.

The fireworks were shot from the baseball diamond at Fairview Park. People usually laid out their blankets and chairs in the surrounding areas ages ahead of time, reserving the best spots. Brit's house backed up to the park, so we always sat in her driveway to watch. The trees had grown taller over the years, so we didn't have quite the same view as when we were younger, but it was tradition.

We sat outside, me and Dash in lawn chairs, Flora and Brit and Terrance sprawled out on the ground. My dad stood at the end of the driveway with Brit's dad, each cradling beers.

I loved the fireworks. The ones that launched into the air with colorful tails, the silence before they burst out into a purple or red or green cloud. The ones that sparked and then flared gold, or screamed in little spirals on the way down. The bright ones that lingered with tendrils shooting out slow, like a big flower blooming in air.

When I was little, I thought that once fireworks went off, all those shiny bits would rain back down to earth like brightly colored coins. And if I could just find them, if I could run to where they fell, I could collect them all up and keep them. I didn't understand that they weren't something you could grasp once they'd been spent. Their existence was temporary—you had to lose them in order to appreciate them.

I thought of August, watching with Kyle and Cadence. They had staked out a spot on the hill sloping down to the baseball field.

I texted him after the fireworks ended. The sky was still filled with smoke.

*What did you think of the show?*

I thought he might not answer for a while, but my phone buzzed immediately.

*A+ fireworks*

And then again:

*I like how the sky looks here*

People often said the stars looked nicer out in the country, that city lights dimmed them.

*Me too*, I replied.


Brit slept over at our house that night.

I paused in front of the dresser while she was down the hall brushing her teeth. I picked up a half-empty perfume bottle sitting atop it, raised it halfway to my face for a smell, then changed my mind and set it down. It'd just stoke that ache in my chest.

I remember when Ciara first left for school. I remember sitting on my bed and looking at Brit sitting across the way on Ciara's.

She had left so much behind, and I couldn't fathom how she could do without her music box, her favorite posters, her stuffed animals.

I remember crossing to the dresser, opening the music box, and watching the princess turn. It still had jewelry inside—a friendship bracelet woven with embroidery thread, a jumble of necklaces, a pair of hoop earrings she had gotten from a girl in her class. It was stuff that would've fit in a suitcase. "How could she leave it?" I murmured. "Like she doesn't even care."

"Maybe it's the opposite," Brit had said. "Maybe it's not like she left it behind because she doesn't care about it. Maybe it's like . . . she left it here so that part of her would still be here, you know? So that this would still be her home, and she'd still have part of it that belongs to her." She had stretched out across the bed, staring up at the ceiling. "And, you know"—she looked over at me—"it means she's coming back."

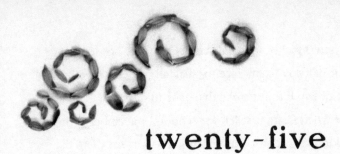

# twenty-five

**Sophie:**

What's your favorite thing about summer?

**Ciara:**

Nooooo schoooooooool

**Sophie:**

Still have to work though

**Ciara:**

True true

But at least they pay me for that

**Sophie:**

What do you like best? In Acadia?

**Ciara:**

The YYS

The Burger Shack
Going out at golden hour
Fireflies
Why do you want to know?

**Sophie:**
Just reminding you of all the great things
For when you get here

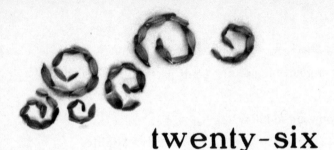

# twenty-six

July continued with band camp—a solid week of all band, all the time. We practiced in sections, we worked on formations, we tried to avoid crashing into one another when executing turns (Chelsea and Becca failed, and took a small portion of the woodwinds section down with them. Brit laughed so hard she crashed into Dash herself, but luckily he was solid enough to keep them both upright). No one passed out from heat this year, but everyone complained about being dehydrated. Terrance kept striking poses to show off how toned his calves were getting from all the marching, and his section leader kept threatening to take his trumpet away if he didn't stop, though the threats rang pretty hollow when she couldn't keep from laughing as his poses got more and more over the top.

After camp, the rehearsal schedule continued, albeit scaled

back a bit. We were preparing for the Midwest Marching Summer Showcase, which would be in Saint Louis partway through the month.

I got a text from August the night before we were set to go:

*You guys are going to stl tomorrow?*

I sent a *yeah* in response. It looked sad on its own, so I started to pick out a string of emojis to send after it, but he answered while I was still curating.

*Dash is driving?*

Seniors could drive separately if they wanted. I thought about the conversation with my mom before dinner—her frowning as she dumped a jar of pasta sauce into a pot.

"Why don't you ride the bus?"

"It's crowded. And loud. We can't listen to our own music. We can't stop for McDonald's."

"Wear headphones. I'll buy you an Egg McMuffin before you leave."

"Mom," I said. "Please."

She "hmmed." I leaned my head against her shoulder.

"Please please please please?"

"You know, repetition isn't a great foundation for a convincing argument. You want to have multiple points to support your claim."

My mom's persuasive-essay assignment was legendary among Acadia Junior High sixth graders. I still remember Brit complaining about it.

"Dash'll be super careful. You know him."

"It's not Dash, it's Brit the Great Distractor I'm worried about."

"I'll be there. I'll mediate."

I ended up winning out. Eventually.

*Yeah*, I texted August, and this time added two thumbs-up emojis before August could reply.

*Can I ride with you guys?*

I blinked.

*You want to come to the showcase?*

He didn't reply immediately. August didn't have an iPhone—neither did I—but I knew that you could see the other person typing if they had an iPhone too. The little bouncing dots that tell you the other person hasn't forgotten you. They're just . . . composing.

I couldn't tell here, though. So maybe August was typing out a long message, or maybe he was typing and retyping a short one, or maybe he had drifted off to sleep—at the late, late hour of 9:00 p.m.—or any other number of scenarios I considered, phone in my hand, until a message finally appeared.

It was much shorter than the pause had implied:

*I mean I can*

That was neither yes nor no. I didn't know what to do with that.

Then he replied again:

*Just want to go home for a minute*

I hadn't even considered it. *Saint Louis is not the big mean city.* Acadia wasn't his home. Saint Louis was. Of course he'd want to go there. It caused something unpleasant to squirm in my stomach, though, however irrational it was.

*Should be no problem*, I said. *Check with Dash though, it's his car.*

166

He didn't reply again.

But he was there in the morning, when we all met in the parking lot at school. We parted ways with Flora and Terrance and piled into the Cutlass—Dash and Brit up front, me and August in the back.

*Not like a double date.*

Brit played deejay, playing songs from her phone since the Cutlass only had a tape deck. We talked a while—me and Brit mostly, with Dash chiming in occasionally—and I didn't notice at first, but next to me, August seemed restless. Distracted. He kept fidgeting more and more as we made our way through the cornfields and the soybean fields and yet more cornfields.

(Brit: "You know what I hate most about it? It's like someone copy-and-pasted the landscape. Just the same sky and the same field over and over again. Like, have some creativity, at least. Break it up with a little flavor every now and then."

Dash: "The billboards add flavor."

Brit: "We clearly have different ideas about flavor, Dashiell.")

August spoke eventually. "Can you pull over up here?"

"Huh?"

"Can you stop? Like at the McDonald's. Please."

Dash didn't comment, just guided the car to the exit ramp like August asked. We parked at the McDonald's, and we were all taking off our seat belts when August said, "I need to borrow the car."

Brit paused, halfway out of her seat. "Are you serious?"

His expression was dead serious. He got out and we joined him on the pavement. "I'll be back, I promise." He looked at Dash. "I won't steal your car, I won't strand you, I swear to God. Just, please, can I borrow it?"

Dash's brow was furrowed. "Why?"

"I . . ." August shook his head. "It's important. I wouldn't ask if it wasn't. Please. I know it's a lot but please trust me."

I thought of Brit's conversation with August on the patio: *I would jump off a bridge if she asked me to. Because I know she wouldn't ask without a really good reason.*

"Please," August said again.

Silence.

And then Dash extended the keys toward him. Something like relief flooded August's face.

"Thank you. Thanks." He took them, and crossed around to the driver's side. "I'll be right back."

We all got food at McDonald's and sat in a booth by the window. It looked out over the attached gas station. Cars and trucks pulled in and out. I watched as a family piled out of a crowded-looking van, stretching like they'd been driving awhile. I wondered where they were headed.

"Where are we even?" Brit said after a few moments of eating.

"Greenville," Dash replied.

"How do you know?" Brit said.

"I'm the driver. I actually, like, read signs and stuff as they go by. I actually keep track of where we're at, if you can believe it."

Brit didn't snark back. She was already on her phone. "Greenville."

She blinked, scrolled, blinked again. "It's the prison, right? The really big one?"

"Do you think—?"

"I mean, he's probably not here to visit"—she scrolled for a moment—"the American Farm Heritage Museum."

"Maybe he's super into farming," I said, though obviously that wasn't true. A gnawing sensation was growing in the pit of my stomach.

"What's his last name again? Shaw?" Brit asked.

"What are you doing?"

"Trying to find out what happened," she replied. "Shaw, Saint Louis, crime. Criminal. Criminal offense."

"Brit."

"Hm?"

"Don't."

She didn't look up, so I put a hand on her wrist, lowered her phone from her face.

"Seriously."

She looked up at me, saw the coinciding *seriously* in my eyes, and clicked off her phone.

"Fine."

Dash went back for more food, and when we got a text from August a while later (*On my way back*), I went up and ordered him a cheeseburger meal, in case he was hungry.

But it was another forty minutes or so until the Cutlass actually appeared in the parking lot. Brit had eaten half the fries I got for August, and the rest were stone-cold. I considered tossing the rest of the meal, but I didn't, crumpling the top of the bag shut and clutching it as I headed out into the parking lot with Brit and Dash trailing behind.

"Thank God," Brit said. "Let's get this show on the road. We're gonna get in trouble if we're late." Our program wasn't until the afternoon, but she was right. It would not go unnoticed if we missed it.

August handed Dash the keys. I handed him the crumpled bag.

"We got you a burger."

His expression was unreadable. "Thanks."

"It might be kinda cold and gross, though. We could order something else?"

He shook his head. "I'll eat it. Thanks."

He didn't say anything after that.

It was a few exits later that August straightened up in his seat.

"Can we stop?"

I could see Dash's frown in the rearview mirror. "Are you serious right now?"

"We just stopped for, like, two hours," Brit said.

"I don't feel good."

"August."

"I'm gonna be sick," he said, with an urgency in his voice that sounded like, yeah, he really might be.

We pulled off and into a gas station and August got out before we'd barely even stopped. I unbuckled my seat belt and followed, watching as he ran from the car to a patch of grass. He was bent over, heaving, when I reached him.

I wanted to rub his back, something, but instead I just stood a few feet away, hands useless at my sides while he made gross sounds. He didn't throw up—just spit a lot.

He straightened up after a while.

"You okay?"

"I don't know why I thought that was a good idea," he said, looking back at me. His eyes were wet.

"I told you that burger would be cold and gross."

He let out a hollow breath of laughter and turned to face the road. Beyond that was the highway, semis and cars zooming by.

"We can pretend it's not happening," I said after a pause. "Or we could talk about it, if you want. If you want to talk, I'll listen."

"What is there to say?"

I shrugged. "Whatever you want."

"I don't know where to start."

I stepped closer. "Were you visiting someone? At Greenville?"

"I didn't even go in," he said. "I couldn't even—I couldn't—" He shook his head. "I'm such a piece of shit, Soph, I couldn't even go in. I tried and I left and I drove back and I tried again but I just . . . I don't know what to say to her."

"Your mom?"

He nodded.

I swallowed. "How long does she have to stay there?"

"Seven years." His face crumpled. He pulled the collar of his T-shirt up over his face.

"I'm sorry," I said, and then said it again, even though I knew how meaningless it was.

One hand still hung by his side, so I reached for it. I could hear Flora's voice in my head—*Laced fingers means it's romantic.* The kind of tidbit she'd share with Brit and me as she pored over dating articles online.

This wasn't the romantic way. It was the same way I'd grab Brit's hand on field trips when we were little kids, a chain of Harrison Elementary kindergartners taking a trip to Fairview Park. One arm pulled ahead of you, one angled back, palms squished in each other's grasp. Brit always insisted on holding my hand and Dash's hand, stretched between the two of us. *Sophie is all-time leader and Dash is all-time caboose.* Dash would stick out his lower lip, eyes sad: *I don't wanna be caboose.*

Brit's gaze was steady. *The caboose is the best part.*

I know if I had complained instead, then the leader would've been the best part. If we were both upset, she'd have found a way to make each part equally good, so long as she got what she wanted—to be buffered on both sides.

Right now I held August's hand. I watched the cars and trucks pass by on the interstate and didn't look over for a while, until August moved to pull his shirt back down. He ran his free hand under his nose.

"I'm okay," he said finally. "It's okay."

It wasn't, but I nodded anyway.

He squeezed my hand once and then let go.

Brit and Dash were standing by the car when we approached, each holding giant Styrofoam cups. Brit handed one to August when we reached them. "It'll settle your stomach," she said.

He took it. "Thanks. Sorry."

Dash was worried, I could tell, but his expression betrayed nothing. "Should we go back?" he said, and then added, "To Acadia," when panic flashed in August's eyes.

"Yeah, fuck the showcase, some Missouri school's gonna sweep the awards anyway," Brit said, before taking a pull from her soda. We all knew we'd be in trouble for ditching, but in this case, I cared as much as they did. Which is to say, not at all.

"No, it's fine," August said. "We should get going. You don't want to miss it."

So we got back in the car and went.

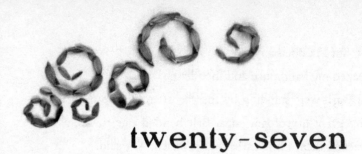

# twenty-seven

The day at the showcase—which stretched into the evening—was long, and everyone was cranky by the end of it. Spending that many hours in plastic seats, outfitted in head-to-toe polyester, isn't ideal, but we made it through.

I didn't like leaving August when we got there. He parted ways with us outside the arena where the showcase was held and said he'd meet us back there before the bus was taking off.

I wanted him to stay. But I didn't know if he would find spending the day in the stands as a spectator to be particularly soothing, so I just watched him as he headed away, down the street and out of sight.

I don't know what he did all day. I texted him—a quick *Going on soon*, a picture of Brit with her hat askew, tongue sticking out, eyes rolled back, captioned *Hot in here*—but he didn't respond.

But he met us at the appointed time that evening all the same, hands shoved in his pockets. It was hot outside too, felt hotter than at home, even as the sun hung low in the sky. The air was thick with humidity.

It grew dark as we drove back. I looked over at August as we neared Greenville, but he was facing the other direction, didn't turn away from the window. Didn't say a word as we neared it, reached it, passed it. Then it was disappearing in the rearview, and we were headed toward Acadia.

I left my hand on the seat next to me, palm up, but he didn't take it.

I watched videos that night, of Megan performing on her season of *America's Next Country Star*.

The full episodes were hard to find online, even cut up into ten-minute chunks on YouTube. But some of Megan's performances had been uploaded, and some compilations of her behind-the-scenes bits had been cut together.

At the start of one in particular—her performance in the first live show of that season—she raised her mic to her lips before the band began, looking up through her lashes at the crowd.

"I want to dedicate this song to everyone in my hometown of Acadia, Illinois. I love you all so much."

She did a rendition of "I Hope You Dance" that brought the house down.

One of the judges—giant cowboy hat, black button-down shirt unbuttoned to mid-chest—leaned back in his chair when she was done. "Megan, how d'you think the people in Acadia will feel about your performance?"

Megan shifted from foot to foot. "I don't know. I just hope they'll be proud of me."

He nodded. "I think they're gonna be real proud."

A smile split her face, wide and radiant.

# twenty-eight

I went over to the Conlins' a few days later. I hadn't seen August since the Saint Louis trip.

He came to the door when I knocked.

"Let's go to Bygones," I said. "Let's go treasure hunting."

He looked at me for a moment. His face betrayed nothing—like Brit when she asked one of her capital-Q Questions, where you would get the eyebrow wrinkle or nothing. But there was some kind of contemplation in his eyes, like he was considering something more significant than a proposition from the world's most average clarinet player.

He nodded. "Okay," he said. "Let's do it."

So we went to Bygones. That was the secret to finding the deals, after all—*You gotta keep coming back around. The inventory's always changing!*

We brushed through the rows of dishes and old silverware; through Mrs. Cabot's booth that may or may not have contained Brit's mom's garbage, and paused in front of a booth in the corner that contained several rows of china dolls, all staring blankly.

I nudged August. "Which one do you think is evil?"

"Do you mean which one do I think is the *most* evil? Because they're all baseline at least a little bit evil."

"Most likely to be found in the empty room of an abandoned house."

He pointed to one with a purple taffeta dress. "That one. For sure."

"Most likely to move in your peripheral vision."

"The one in the red." She had porcelain-white skin and deep-red lips pursed in a Mona Lisa kind of smile. "Obviously. Look at her. That's some sinister shit right there. You move, she moves."

I huffed a laugh.

"Did you have any creepy murder dolls when you were little?" August said a few booths down as we poked through a box of old black-and-white photos.

"Nah. Flora got one from her dad when we were pretty young, but she wasn't allowed to play with it. Probably for the best—Brit definitely would've destroyed it."

We flipped through the pictures in silence for a moment. Photos of two young women with cat-eye glasses. A man and a woman standing in front of a truck. A baby in a little playsuit and shiny black shoes.

When August spoke, his voice was striving for neutral. Casual. "Did you ever know your dad? Like your birth dad?"

"No." I didn't think often on the man who was my father, because he wasn't, really. My dad—the one who had carved pumpkins with me, taught me to skate, braided my hair badly but painstakingly when I was a little kid—he was the only dad I'd ever known. Dad prime. All-time Dad.

"He left before I was born," I said.

August turned away from the pictures, moving toward a shelf of knickknacks. "Doesn't that make you mad, though? Like . . . not even at him, because screw him, but like . . . at the universe, you know? Because why should you have to be left alone like that?"

This was as close as we'd touch to the Saint Louis trip—standing at the gas station, August's shoulders shaking.

"I'm not alone, though," I said carefully. "I never was. I've always had my mom, and my dad, and Ciara. And anyway, it happened. It's already done. There's nothing I can do to change it. So why would I spend time feeling shitty about something I can't change?"

It was quiet for a moment. "I knew you'd say something like that," he said. "Since you're a good person and all."

"I'm not any better than anyone else."

"But you care about people. Like . . . more than most people do."

"How do you know?"

"You make Cadence mac and cheese on the stove."

"What does that have to do with anything?"

"The microwave kind is so much faster. The kind from the box means you have to boil the water and cook the pasta and make the sauce and mix it together. It takes longer and it tastes a thousand times better and that's the kind you make for her, because you care. You do what's better, even if it's harder."

"Easy Mac isn't hard," I murmured. "It literally has 'easy' in the name."

"You know what I mean," he replied.

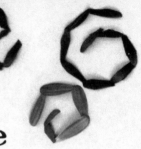

# twenty-nine

**Sophie:**

What should we do first when you get here?

**Ciara:**

Can I call you right now?

Do you have time to talk?

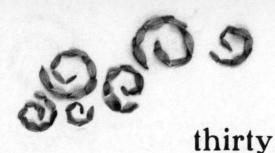

# thirty

Friday night found us back at Tegan's house—inside this time—
sitting around talking about band stuff, which I easily navigated into
talking about Megan.

"I think we should probably get tickets soon for her concert at
the state fair," I said. I had been compulsively checking every few
days, just to make sure they were still available. "So we should figure out who's going."

"Well, Dash'll drive, so there's one," Brit said, settling down next
to him on the couch with a newly filled cup.

Dash looked up from his phone. "You know, everyone always
assumes I'm gonna drive. What if I have plans?"

"Do you?"

"I could."

"I'll drive," I said.

"I'll do it, I'm just saying," Dash replied, tapping out something on his phone.

Brit leaned into him. "Tell your man we say hi. Tell him you say—" She started making kissing sounds by Dash's ear.

"Can you not?" he said.

"Did you get all that?" She made several more kissing sounds.

"*Anyway*," I said, before she could do any more Foley work. "It's on the seventeenth. So just let me know. If you want to go." I glanced at August.

"Where is it?" he asked.

"In Springfield."

"How far?"

"Like two and a half hours?"

"So the radius of how close she'll come to Acadia is max two and a half hours."

Terrance nodded. He had settled on the floor as well. "She couldn't declare the state of Illinois entirely dead to her, or else she could never play Chicago."

"You know, I've been doing some reading—" I began.

"Of course you have," Brit interjected.

"Old articles and stuff, and watching videos, going way back. It just seemed like she loved it here so much, before everything. Like before she actually got famous. I just don't get why she wouldn't want to come back."

"Yeah because if it were up to you, we'd all just stay in Acadia," Brit said.

"Because Acadia is the best place in the world."

"Is it? Is it really? Do you really love having to drive forty minutes just to get to Walmart? Do you super love the isolation? Screw that, do you love how small-minded and racist people can be sometimes?"

"There isn't racism in Acadia."

"Sophie." Brit gave a harsh bark of a laugh. "Fuck. Just because you've never experienced something doesn't mean it's not happening."

I blinked.

"All that being said, I gotta wonder, how can you know it's the best place in the world when you've never even *been* anywhere?"

"I've been places," I said.

She kept right on going. "Look, I know how it's gonna go. You're gonna go to school as close as you can, and when you're finished, you'll move back and get a job and live here for the rest of your life and die and be buried at Oak Hill cemetery and fertilize the very earth of the town you love so much. But not everyone wants that, Soph, not everyone is happy being mediocre. Just look at Ciara. She wanted to get out."

I didn't speak.

"Brit," Flora said softly, at the same time August said:

"You're wrong."

Brit didn't look his way, but instead blinked at me slowly, and then shook her head. "I didn't mean—"

"You're wrong," August repeated, and turned to me. "There's nothing wrong with wanting that. It's not mediocre."

I nodded. "I, uh." I gestured backward, like that could convey *I'm going to the restroom.* Then I left.

Sometimes you just can't help but think of the bad things. Sometimes something sparks it, like kindling, and suddenly they catch, one igniting another, random and unavoidable.

I thought about being four and losing the seashell I had brought to school for show-and-tell, the one my mom had lent me. I thought about being eight and Brit daring me to sneak a peek at the dead deer in Mr. Cabot's garage, hanging from a beam wrapped in a sheet, blood flowing down the driveway. I thought about Ciara's voice at the other end of the line:

*I just . . . I know it sucks, but I just don't think I'm gonna make it back this summer. I think it's better if I stay put.*

*But you said—*

*Sophie—*

*You said that we'd spend the summer together!*

It was the only way I could bear the idea of her leaving. She promised that she'd be back and we'd do all our favorite things, that come summer it would be like nothing had changed.

*I'm making more money here, I can save more, and my roommates need—*

*Ciara!*

*—and Ravi—*

*You said!*

*I'm sorry.*

I squeezed my eyes shut and listed my schools in my mind. Community colleges. State schools. Private universities.

Likelihood of acceptance. Likelihood of financial aid.

Distance from Acadia.

August was standing in the hall when I emerged from the bathroom.

"Everything okay?" he said.

"Never been better."

He smiled a little, tentatively. "Yeah?"

I smiled too, because what else was there to do? Cry? What would that accomplish? I'd feel some kind of release maybe. August would just feel awkward.

"Yeah," I said. "This is the peak of human existence right here."

"Right here in this hallway."

"Right here, in this hallway, at the best party currently happening on planet Earth."

"Is it?"

"You didn't know?"

His smile slipped a little. Maybe mine wasn't as convincing as I thought.

"You sure you're okay?"

I shrugged. "Brit's just drunk."

"That's not an excuse to be a dick."

"She just says shit sometimes. She doesn't mean any harm."

"That's not an excuse either, if what you're saying still hurts people."

I looked off down the hall. I didn't know what to say to that.

He took a step closer. "Sophie . . ."

I met his eyes. He looked so serious. It drew a real smile from me this time, small but genuine nonetheless. "August."

He was regarding me closely, a complicated look in his eyes. "You have something on your face," he said finally, and I touched my fingers to my mouth, but he shook his head. He moved closer and reached out a hand, resting his fingertips lightly against the side of my face, looking intently as he brushed his thumb against my cheek.

"Did you get it?" I murmured.

"I might have made it up," he murmured back. "Sorry."

I huffed a laugh. "At least you're honest." My voice was hushed, even though we were all alone, even though there was no one around to listen. "Or. Half honest." I swallowed, and my gaze dropped to his lips. "You know . . . you have something on your mouth."

His smile was the last thing I saw before my eyes slipped shut.

It wasn't like that first kiss, the first of many on the blanket in the field. *Just for research, okay?* and then a switch flipped from Decidedly Not Kissing to Enthusiastically Making Out. I couldn't catalog the start and finish of the first one, because it ran so fluidly into the second and the third and the fourth.

This one was a soft press of lips to start, barely parted, the lightest bit of pressure, and then we pulled back for a moment. I looked up at him, but his eyes were turned downward. His eyelashes were unfairly long.

Then we kissed again. And again. And so on, slow and deliberate, each one growing longer, each one spreading through me. This was kissing, but it felt a little like talking too. Like *I like you* and *You make me laugh* and *I want you to feel good, I want to make you feel good—*

I threaded my fingers through his hair, and he wrapped his arms around my waist, and we talked, or didn't, until a door opened up at the end of the hall.

We froze as a couple emerged, laughing and talking, and walked right past us.

August pulled back and looked at me, eyebrows raised in question.

I slipped my hand in his, and pulled him toward the open door.

It was happening again, the slow slide of time, same as the first time in that respect, but different in that this felt . . . purposeful. This was building, moving toward something.

The pillows on the bed were too soft; it was like sinking into a cloud. August slipped a hand behind my head—like he knew—and kissed me deeper, meanwhile his other hand slipped under my shirt, resting tentatively at the dip of my waist.

"This okay?" he murmured between kisses.

"Yeah." My voice stuck in my throat. "Yes," I said as he traced higher and higher on my rib cage. I didn't know where I wanted to touch him beyond *everywhere*. I didn't know how to narrow that down, what to focus on when it all felt like so much.

"August."

"Hm?"

He pulled back. His lips were red, wet with spit.

*I just wanted to say your name.* Could I even say that? Was it too much? Jesus, I was in deep.

He looked at me for a moment, and then swallowed, and something was happening behind his eyes that I couldn't decipher.

He rolled over suddenly and sat up, swinging his legs around and placing his feet on the floor.

"No, don't stop," I said. "I didn't—That's not what I—" I sat up too, scooted toward him. I wanted to reach for him, to press kisses to the line of his shoulders, but I didn't. I rested my hands on my knees, just to hold off.

"I—" He didn't turn around. "I'll be right back, okay?"

"What are you—"

But before I could finish the question, he was across the room, slipping out the door and shutting it softly.

I waited.

For a while I still felt the pulse of blood through me, warmth high in my cheeks and elsewhere. I also felt, increasingly, the irrational desire to burst into tears.

I don't know how people did it—making out, hooking up— because to me, being with someone that way seemed to bring every possible emotion right to the surface. I felt unbearably vulnerable in moments like that, whereas Brit viewed it more like a recreational activity. Like Ping-Pong, or online gaming. I envied her. I was an open nerve. I didn't know how to be exposed like that.

I adjusted my shirt. Fussed with my hair in the mirror over the dresser. The longer I waited, the more I knew August wasn't coming back, but I also knew that the moment I went downstairs, it would be an actual fact that actually existed, a thing that genuinely happened. August Shaw kissed me. And then he left me.

Eventually I opened the door. Stepped into the hallway and

moved to the top of the stairs. The floorboards creaked under my feet, but it was too loud downstairs to draw any notice.

August was there, right there in the front hallway at the bottom of the stairs, standing at the half-open door with Terrance and a few girls from the color guard.

Terrance had his arms raised in the air, in the middle of some story, and the girls were laughing. August grinned, and I wanted to say it looked distracted, like it didn't quite reach his eyes, but that would be a lie. It looked the way it always looked—happy and roguish, almost too big for his face.

He leaned into Terrance and said something to him, and Terrance turned and clapped one hand into August's.

My thoughts battled it out:

*He's heading this way. He's coming back up.*

*No he's not. Fuck that, call his name, make a scene.*

*I just wanted to say your name.*

*I just wanted . . .*

I watched as August left, the front door shutting behind him with a definitive *click.*

# thirty-one

I watched Megan Pleasant videos that night.

I wasn't in the mood for performances—didn't think I could handle a lovesick ballad—so I focused on interviews, bouncing from one to the next in the recommended-videos section.

I eventually came across a clip of a sixteen-year-old Megan at some minor award show red carpet.

"My first red carpet ever. Ever! Can you believe?"

"Megan, you look incredible, tell us about what you're wearing."

Megan described her outfit, and then smiled at the presenter. "You look really pretty too."

The presenter, stick-thin and bigheaded, turned to the camera, blinking heavily smoky-eyed lids. "Isn't she just a sweetheart? That's what everyone says about you, honey. You are so genuine, and it's so refreshing, lemme tell you."

Megan beamed at the camera. "Thank you."

"Now, your new single, 'Always You,' from your debut album is out now. Loved the video for that, by the way. Gorgeous stuff."

"Thank you. You're so nice."

"I've got some lyrics here—'Dreaming of you always, thinking of you always' . . . 'You say I'm your queen, I say you're my ace of hearts' . . . Now we all know, you write all your own stuff, you're this amazing singer-songwriter, so I gotta know . . . who's the inspiration behind this? Who's your ace of hearts?"

"Oh, you know. Creative license and all that."

"Somebody back home? Hometown sweetheart?"

Megan just gave a little shrug, one dimple popping out on a smile.

The video for "Always You" came up next, autoplay cycling right into a scene of Megan in a beautiful white flowing dress, walking through a misty field. Strumming a guitar at the base of a tree. Standing at the edge of a pond, her bare feet in the shallows as she sang:

"'Thinking of you always, looking for you always, your laugh on the wind, your light in the sky . . .'

"'Hoping for you always.'"

I shut the video off.

# thirty-two

**Ciara:**

I saw another mullet!!!!!!!!!

It wasn't even 10% ironic

Amazing

**Ciara:**

Work is sooooo boring.

How's band stuff going?

**Ciara:**

Okay new idea:

What do you think about visiting me??

I think I could get mom and dad on board

We could pool our money for a ticket

And ask for advanced Christmas and birthday presents

　　lolol

Maybe in August?

There's lots of fun stuff we could do here


**Ciara:**

ANOTHER MULLET I SWEAR TO GOD

Is this a thing?

Are they coming back?

How much would you pay me if I convinced Ravi to

　　get one?


**Ciara:**

I talked to mom about the visit

What do you think? Are you super busy?

Just let me know what you think


**Ciara:**

Hope band and stuff is going okay

Miss you lots

# thirty-three

It's not that I was avoiding everyone on purpose. But I picked up some extra shifts over the next few days. I dived into SAT prep as per *The College Collective*'s recommendation. I didn't go by Teen Zone 2. And I didn't see August either.

Not until Wednesday evening. I was riding my bike back from work, and he was getting out of the car with Kyle as I pedaled up to our driveway.

We made eye contact, so it was impossible to get away without at least acknowledging each other.

"Be there in a minute," August told Kyle, and then crossed the lawn to where I stood. "Hey," he said.

"Hey, stranger." I tried to smile. I could be totally normal.

"How's it going?"

I shrugged. "I had work tonight. There was this whole expired coleslaw fiasco."

"Cool." It was like he hadn't even heard what I said, like he had rehearsed what he was going to say so my responses were negligible. "So, uh. Look. About the other night—"

He paused here, like he was expecting me to interrupt. *It's okay,* or *Nah, forget about it.* But I just blinked at him.

August smiled a little, forced sheepishness. "I, uh, I was pretty drunk," he said, shoving his hands in his pockets, looking off down the street. "Don't really . . . like I wasn't really thinking about . . . what I was doing . . ."

Something dropped in the pit of my stomach, hard like a stone. "I didn't know that. I wouldn't have . . . I'd never . . ."

The fake smile evaporated, and a wrinkle appeared between his brows. "What?"

"If you were drunk, then we shouldn't have done anything. I didn't know, I would never—"

He shook his head. "I wasn't that drunk," he said, frowning. "I actually . . . wasn't drunk at all, okay?"

"Which was it, were you or weren't you?"

"I wasn't." He met my eyes. "I was just trying to make it . . . less . . ."

Oh.

*You . . . seem really nice.* He had said it all at the Movie Dome, what felt like ages ago. My mom always said, *Given the chance, people will tell you exactly how they feel. You just have to be willing to listen.* And August had told me. He had. I don't know why I was surprised.

"It's fine," I said. "We don't have to talk about it anymore."

"Sophie—"

"I would like it if we acted like it never happened. Okay?"

I didn't wait for a response. I gripped the handlebars of my bike harder, started walking it toward the garage.

"Soph, wait."

I looked back.

"Can we—Are we still okay? Like are we friends?"

"I don't know," I said, and he looked inexplicably upset. That made me angrier. He didn't have the right to be upset. His eyes shouldn't be the ones going sad, his mouth turned down at the corners.

"Friends don't lie to each other," I continued. "Or say they're drunk if they're not. Or say they'll be right back and then never come back. They don't do that to each other."

He opened his mouth to speak, let out a breath instead, looked away, looked back. "I'm . . . sorry," he said finally. "I didn't mean to hurt you. I wasn't trying to."

"Don't give yourself so much credit," I replied, and walked away. He didn't stop me.

I stowed my bike in the garage and paused at the back door, squeezing my eyes shut against the prickle of tears. I thought about texting Ciara: *This sucks, everything sucks, wanna call, wanna come visit.*

I told myself she wouldn't have experience in this kind of thing anyway. Ciara didn't date until she got to college—not that this was dating, or anything close to dating. She met Ravi at their freshman orientation, and that was it.

*I have met a very cute boy, Sophie.*

The Very Cute Boy became her boyfriend.

I liked Ravi. We talked on the phone occasionally. His parents had moved from India to the US, and he was born in Maryland. He liked tabletop gaming and rock climbing, and he was always quoting depressing British sitcoms that he insisted were funny. He wanted to go to grad school like Ciara, to study biology.

Maybe Ravi had done stupid things in their relationship—I wouldn't know. Maybe he and Ciara both had. But they were in a relationship, a real one, whereas August and I were nothing.

That much was clear.

# thirty-four

That night I read a profile of Megan from a few years ago, just before her third album was set to release. It was one of the many I had sent to WWYSE over the last few weeks, to little result. I had almost resigned myself to the fact that no one was going to be as into the Megan Pleasant mission as I was, but it didn't hurt to try.

I skimmed the description of the album, the facts about Megan and her start on *America's Next Country Star*, to get to the meat of it.

> *Pleasant cites traveling and meeting new people as two of the best parts of being famous. "Being able to take care of my family a little, that's really nice too." Pleasant's parents recently moved to Nashville, while her only brother, Connor, is a freshman at Indiana University.*

As for the worst parts of fame, Pleasant is not short on thoughts: "Sometimes it feels like people expect you to be different. Like there's this notion that you're not a real person anymore. That you don't like the same things you liked before, or even feel things the same way everyone else does. But I feel the same on the inside. I still want McDonald's breakfast sometimes, you know? I still watch Friends reruns before bed. I still get nervous before a performance. I'm not different inside just because people know who I am. It still hurts if someone says I suck at singing. It still feels good when someone says that my music has helped them in some way."

I mention the theory in physics that posits that by observing a phenomenon, you've inherently changed it. Does it not apply here? Pleasant doesn't disagree. "I'm not saying it hasn't changed me at all. Of course it has. I just mean, people think it makes you into something else. Something above—or below even, I don't know— just something apart from everyone else. I'm different, yeah, but like the core of me and who I am and what I think and feel is the same as it was before. And I'll be the same when all of this is over."

It bears noting that Pleasant has often spoken in absolutes over the course of her career. ANCS was "the best possible introduction to the industry" she could have had. Her hometown of Acadia is "the best small town in the world, bar none." Here, the absolute is marked—it's not if this ends, it's when all of this is over. As if it's a certainty.

"My mom always says you have to know when to leave the party," Pleasant says. But with two gold-certified albums, three CMA *nominations, and a hint of Grammy buzz for* Foundation *under her belt, it seems like for Pleasant, the party continues. At least for now.*

My phone dinged late that evening. A message from Brit, although it wasn't in the chat.

*Megan's brother goes to IU, right?*

*Yeah,* I replied. *But how do you know that?*

*It was in one of those articles you sent us*

*You read them?*

*Don't sound so shocked*

She was trying to apologize, I think. For the thing at the party. I started to type a response but a string of messages popped up:

*I've got a lead*

*His friends are throwing a party in Bloomington on Saturday*

*He'll be there*

*Got all the details*

I responded with a run of exclamation points.

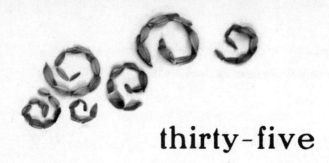

# thirty-five

It was about two hours to Bloomington from Acadia. I told my parents I was going to Brit's, and that I'd probably sleep over. I felt bad lying, and told Brit so as we sat on her front steps, waiting for Dash. She had a duffel bag at her side.

"That's good," she replied.

"Why?"

"If you feel bad about it, it means you're still a good person."

"I don't think it works like that."

"No, it does. How can you know you're a good person if you're never tested?" She knocked her shoulder against mine. "We should all lie more often, just to make sure."

Dash pulled up with August in the passenger's seat.

Brit stood, saying "Nuh-uh, nope, no way," like she was voicing my inner monologue. For one brief moment I thought maybe she knew what had happened between us, despite the fact that I hadn't told anyone. "Not gonna fly."

She approached the car and opened August's door. "Back seat, buddy. I called shotgun for all time."

August didn't put up a fight, just got out and glanced at me as he moved to the back seat. I was still standing on the front steps of Brit's house. I wanted a whole lot more space between August and me than a back seat could provide.

But I couldn't explain that—why he absolutely couldn't come with us—without explaining the whole thing. So I just got in the car.

"What are you doing here?" I said as we made our way toward the interstate, and Brit began to queue up road-trip music.

He shrugged, his expression neutral. "Felt like coming along."

"Why?"

"Why not? It's not every day you get to meet Megan Pleasant's brother."

I didn't reply.

Brit asked Dash to stop at a gas station outside town, "so we can change for the party."

I hadn't brought anything special to wear, but apparently that was what was in Brit's duffel.

She emerged from the bathroom stall wearing a short skirt and a sparkly top that was little more than a scrap of sequined fabric that tied around the neck and across the back.

"Where did you get that?"

"My mom," Brit said. "It was her 'going out' top back in the day."

I raised my eyebrows. "And she gave it to you? To wear?"

A shrug. "She didn't say *not* to wear it." Her face was already made up—"Flora did it," she told me, when I commented. "She should've done yours too."

"I didn't know we were being fancy," I replied, though *fancy* wasn't quite the right word.

"You could do something with your shirt." She stepped behind me, grabbed the hem of my T-shirt in the back and bunched up the fabric, twisting it up and under in the back so an expanse of stomach was now revealed.

August and Dash said nothing when we walked out.

We made it into town as the sun was setting, and followed the directions to the address Brit had found. People were standing in front of the house as we approached, cars lining the street on both sides.

"We can't all go in," Brit said as Dash passed the place and turned the corner, looking for a place to park.

"Why not?" Dash said.

"It's gonna be way easier for two girls to talk their way into this kind of thing than two guys."

August frowned. "I think we should go too."

"Trust me"—Brit popped her door open as Dash slowed to a stop at the next corner—"we'll be in and out."

We got inside without anyone stopping us.

It was all pounding bass, a crush of people, each group talking louder than the next to be heard. I scanned the room as we edged through the crowd to get into the living room.

I'd seen pictures of Connor Pleasant from back in the day—a skinny, gawky kid posing next to Megan in front of a banner for the *America's Next Country Star* live shows. It was hard to find anything recent; his Instagram was private.

"You'll probably recognize him better," I said to Brit. "How'd you get him to add you, anyway?"

Brit was looking around too, but it didn't seem like she was listening. She grabbed my shoulder all of a sudden, leaned in to speak in my ear.

"Don't be mad."

"Sorry?"

"Connor isn't here."

I blinked. "What?"

"I lied. He's not here. I'm sorry."

"What—why—"

Brit looked right at me, eyes lined dark all around, lashes thick with mascara. Her going-out top caught the overhead light and winked at me. "Because I needed you here for this."

"For what?"

Brit's eyes left me, scanning the room.

"Brit."

Her focus landed on a cluster of guys in the corner.

I reached for her wrist. "Brit, I swear—"

She moved away before I could grab hold of her, cutting quickly across the room.

By the time I caught up, she was already in conversation with one of the guys. The others looked my way as I joined the group.

"This is Jenny," Brit said, gesturing to me. "We're gonna be roommates."

"Freshmen?"

Brit nodded, and the guys laughed. "Starting early, huh?" and "Cool cool cool" and "How'd you get in here?"

"We can be super persuasive." Brit's eyes were glassy like she was level-three drunk. Her gaze kept darting toward a lean, blond guy holding a can of beer. I had never met him, but I knew for certain—it was Tanner Barnes.

Brit started chatting with him, meanwhile, one of his friends kept trying to engage me in conversation.

His fourth or fifth try: "So . . . what are you gonna major in?"

"Um . . . education, probably." I wanted to grab Brit's sleeve, but there were no sleeves to tug on. I settled for wrapping a hand around her wrist, leaning in close to speak: "Hey, I think we should go."

She pulled away from me, lurched toward Tanner.

"So you're on the track team, huh?"

"Uh-huh. Yeah." He took a long pull from his beer.

"I do track too."

"Yeah?"

"Uh-huh. Let's race."

He was drunk already, getting drunker. But he smiled. "Yeah okay. We could race back to my place."

"A hundred meters," Brit said.

"For real?" The smile widened.

"Yeah." Brit smiled too, teeth gleaming, and she swayed closer toward him. I alone knew she was stone-cold sober. "I bet you're fast."

"Well, not all the time," he said. "Like not with everything. Don't want you to get the wrong idea, if you know what I mean."

She laughed, and it sounded like a stranger's laugh, like someone I hadn't known all my life. "For sure. But I wanna see how fast you can go. Then you can show me . . . how you take it slow."

Brit would punch Brit for saying something that stupid. But she was possessed right now. And this was a bad, bad, bad idea.

"Okay, let's do it." Tanner pounded the rest of his drink back.

"A hundred meters," she said again.

"Are we going like regulation here or what?"

"Fuck yeah we're going regulation." She grabbed his hand, leading him away.

"What dorm are you guys gonna be in?" Tanner's friend said to me.

"Sorry," I replied, and went after them.

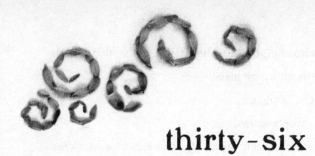

# thirty-six

Brit somehow convinced Tanner to take us to the university track. "I wanna see it!" she said, and "It's on the way to our place," smiling coyly at him and studiously ignoring me.

We made it to the track and managed to get in, Brit flirting with Tanner all along.

"I'll time you," I said, and headed down to the 100-meter mark. Instead of bringing up the timer, I first tapped out a quick text:

*We are at the IU track please come pick us up*

*Brit is doing something stupid*

Dash's reply came instantly, as I brought up the timer.

*On our way*

I called out the ready, set, go, and they took off.

It was only a matter of seconds, but you could see exactly when

Tanner realized Brit was good. He was half-assing it to start, but he pushed forward, lengthening his stride, increasing his speed for the final seconds. It wasn't enough to close the distance between them as Brit crossed the 100-meter mark first.

They kept going after, propelled by their own momentum. *You can't just stop dead when you go that fast*, Brit told me once. *You can't just turn it on and off like a faucet.*

He said something to her as they slowed to a stop, a grin breaking his flushed face. I watched as he reached out, snaking his arms around Brit's waist.

She turned and wrenched out of his grip. Punched him in the stomach once, and as he doubled over, shoved him to the ground.

I moved quickly, running toward them, grabbing Brit around the middle and pulling her back before she could do anything more. She struggled against me as Tanner wheezed.

"The fuck," he choked out.

"That was for Luke." Brit's voice was tight, tears streaming down her face.

"The hell is wrong with you?"

"You ruined it, you ruined everything," she said, trying to pull out of my grip, but I held fast.

"Brit, stop."

We were alone, it was dark, and even though he was drunk and momentarily down for the count, Tanner Barnes could get his feet back under him at any moment, and I didn't want to be there when he did.

"What the fuck?" He rolled onto his side, moving to get up.

"Brit." I stepped backward, pulling her with me. "We're going. Right now."

I grabbed her hand and we ran.

Away from the track, out onto the street. It was Brit who pulled up first, her hand slipping from my grip.

She sat down abruptly on the curb, face streaked with tears, expression blank.

"You can't do this right now." I tried to pull her back up, but she refused to move, refused to look at me. "We have to get out of here, okay?" My pulse was punching fast, my lungs tightening.

And then the Cutlass pulled up. August hopped out of the passenger's side before it had even come to a full stop.

"What happened? Are you okay?"

"She won't get up." I gestured hopelessly to Brit as Dash got out of the driver's side and circled around. "We saw Tanner Barnes, she freaked out. We have to get out of here—"

"It's okay." Dash knelt down in front of Brit.

"Who's Tanner Barnes?" August asked.

"Remember Coach Junior?" I replied. "He made it happen, it was him." Luke, the roof, the fall—or the jump, really, but *jump* sounds intentional and *fall* sounds accidental and what happened to Luke was an unfair mix of both.

Brit turned her face up to Dash, mascara running down her cheeks. She reached up both arms and he picked her up easily, like a little kid, and carried her to the car. August opened the door to the back seat and Dash set her inside.

"Hey!"

I spun around. Tanner Barnes was lumbering toward us.

"Yeah, you. What the fuck?"

August moved toward him, and Dash straightened up from the back seat, snapping Brit's door shut and then tossing me the keys.

I was torn. Brit needed me, and we needed to get out of here, but if there was going to be a fight—a confrontation, an anything—I wanted to help.

"Can I help you?" August intercepted Tanner, his tone bright. "Are you lost? Do you need me to call you a ride?"

Dash strode toward them, taller than both, his hands in loose fists at his sides.

I hesitated a moment, and then got in the car.

I glanced at Brit in the rearview mirror as I started the engine. Her eyes were shut, her head tipped back.

Outside, Tanner was now pushing into August's space, shouting something; Dash was edging between them.

I hated the sound of yelling. I didn't want to see anyone get hurt. I didn't want anyone to get in trouble. I desperately wanted to be home in bed with the fan on, looking over at Ciara's side of the room—you could change what was over there, but it would always be her side of the room—even if it made me sad. I wanted to hear the TV from the living room, the low murmur of my parents' conversation: *Five letters, "not a whit." Four letters, "almost fall."* The wanting was so strong, I could hardly remember why we came here in the first place, I could hardly think of a way out of it.

Until I eased the car up alongside them and laid on the horn, blaring long and loud and unforgiving.

Tanner jerked back. Dogs started barking. I didn't let up as August and Dash retreated. August hopped into the passenger side, Dash in the back.

I sped off, leaving Tanner in the street, fuming. Or at least I assumed. Didn't have much time to assess as he was disappearing in the rearview mirror.

*Lord help me, I'm never going back.*

# thirty-seven

The trip back to Acadia was nothing like the trip down. Blasting Brit's road-trip music, the anticipation of finally making headway on the Megan Pleasant mission.

This was muted, the road stretching out, dark on either side except for the illumination of our headlights.

I could hear Dash murmuring to Brit every now and then, but otherwise it was silent. Until August said, "So . . . fun night?"

"Don't."

"What? I'm serious. That dude? Super charming."

I didn't reply.

"Wish I could've been there when Brit kicked his ass," he muttered after a moment. "Getting his phone was somewhat satisfying, though."

"What?"

"Nicked it," he said, and when I looked over, he was holding a shiny gold phone. "Just in case."

"What? Why? Why would you do that?"

August shrugged. "In case Brit wanted to blackmail him or something. I have to figure out how to unlock it, but you know there's got to be some kind of embarrassing shit on there."

I pounded the heel of my hand against the steering wheel. "You can't just take people's stuff!"

"Well, apparently he took Brit's brother's future first, so . . ."

"We have to go back."

"What?"

"We have to give it back. We can . . . put it in his mailbox or something."

"I know exactly where I want to put it and it's not his mailbox."

"I swear to God—"

"Will you both just shut up?" Dash rumbled. The headlights from a passing car lit up the interior for a moment, and I could see Brit in the back seat, tucked into Dash's side, expression vacant and unfixed.

"It's a crime, August," I said, trying to keep my voice under control. "You could get arrested. You could go to *jail*. You think you'd be the first person concerned about that."

I didn't have to look over—I could feel August's eyes on me. After a beat, a silence nearly too thick for the car to contain, I heard the crank of the window being lowered. The Cutlass didn't have automatic windows.

"Fine," August said, and then tossed the phone out.

I slammed on the brakes.

"Why would you do that?"

He didn't respond. He was looking down at where I had thrown my arm out to stop him from hitting the dashboard.

I dropped my hand, placed it back on the steering wheel, and eased the car onto the shoulder. Parked, unclicked my seat belt, got out of the car.

"What are you doing?"

I slammed the door and started marching resolutely back in the direction we had come.

Another door slammed, and footsteps fell in behind me.

"This is stupid. You're being stupid."

"You are," I said, in possibly the weakest comeback of all time, but I couldn't help it. My head was pulsing, tears building behind my eyes. "You don't *think*, you just *do stuff*, without stopping to think about how it might affect people—"

"I know exactly how this is gonna affect him—he can't call Ubers or send people pictures of his dick. What a tragedy."

I stopped, my sneakers grinding to a halt against the pavement. I squeezed my eyes shut and several hot tears slipped down my cheeks fast, the heavy, stinging kind, dripping off my jaw and splattering on my shirt.

"Look, I know you care about everybody but maybe don't extend it to that jaghole," he continued, until I looked back at him, and his brow softened immediately with something like confusion.

"What are you doing?" he said.

"We have to find the phone," I replied, trying to suppress the waver in my voice.

"We're just—arguing." He shook his head minutely. "We're just saying stupid stuff like people do. Right?" He stepped toward me. "Because I'm . . . because I suck, and you said the jail thing, and that was . . . pretty accurate, and I just . . . I . . ."

"We have to find the phone," I repeated, scanning the ground, gone blurry with tears.

When I glanced up again, he was still looking at me, face thrown in relief in the light from the nearby telephone pole. After a moment, he nodded.

"Yeah, okay."

We found the phone. Scattered in pieces along the side of the road.

We both stood and stared down at it, like we were looking into an open grave. August had his hands in his pockets.

"Well," he said.

I shook my head. The tears had dried up. Mostly I just felt . . . empty.

"It's fine. It's whatever."

"You were right. I shouldn't have taken it."

"I don't feel like you actually even think that."

"I mean, I definitely think he's an asshole who deserves to have his phone crushed into a million pieces. But. I feel bad."

"No, you don't."

His voice was soft. "I feel bad that you feel bad. I don't . . . ever want to do anything that makes you feel bad."

I laughed. It was brittle.

"What?"

"Nothing." I shrugged. "Just. You're so full of shit you don't even realize how full of shit you are."

"What do you mean?"

"Why did you kiss me?"

"I didn't."

"Fine. We kissed each other. But still."

"We didn't. It didn't happen, remember?"

"August, I swear—"

"It was for research."

"It wasn't." I couldn't help the break in my voice. "Don't bullshit me, okay? Just be serious for like one second."

"Because I wanted to," he replied. "Because I couldn't not."

"Then why did you leave?" I blinked hard, willing more tears away. "I felt . . . really bad. I felt like an idiot, and you just . . . you didn't even care."

"It's not—" He shook his head. "I did. I do." When I met his gaze, there was something pleading in his expression. "You're . . . my best friend, Sophie."

I didn't speak.

"You're my best friend, and nothing here is gonna last."

"What do you mean?"

He looked away, and when he spoke, it was halting: "I can't stay here. With Kyle and Heather. I can't stay."

"What? Why?"

He just shook his head again.

"August."

"You know I never even met Kyle until everything with my mom? But he and Heather have given me a place to stay, and food, and clothes, and it's . . . They're so kind, but they've got Cady and Harper and I won't be a burden to them. They don't owe me anything. So . . . as soon as I turn eighteen, I'm going to leave. That was . . . that's been my plan from the start."

The information slotted into place. "They won't . . . It's not like they'd kick you out. They would never do that."

"Yeah because they're too nice. They're good people. So I'm gonna make it easy on them." It was quiet for a moment. "And that's . . . that's why I can't join the band, I can't make plans for the fall, I can't . . . be a boyfriend, or . . . anything, and I'm sorry, I wish—" He swallowed. "I wish I could. Like, I really do. You have no idea how much."

"You just want to leave here and be totally on your own?"

"No, but . . . it'll be for the best—"

"You don't want anyone looking out for you?"

"I would, but—"

"You don't want to finish school?"

"I do. But—"

"But what? Your plan is stupid. You're part of their family. You're already—you won't stop meaning something to—to us, just because you think you're temporary—"

He didn't reply. Just stood there, and after a moment, knelt down and picked through a couple of pieces of the phone rubble.

"I'll get a new phone and mail it to him," he said quietly. "Or maybe not a new one, but . . . some refurbished shit online or something. We'll get his address from Brit, she obviously knew how to track him down." He straightened up and looked back at the car. "I would never mess with her."

"I've never seen her like this," I murmured, but that was a lie. I had.

August looked at me for a moment more, his expression unreadable.

"Let's go," I said, before he could speak again.

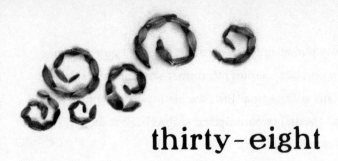

# thirty-eight

.

When we were twelve and Flora was eleven, Brit and Flora got into a huge argument.

This was nothing special. Flora and Brit got into arguments all the time—some big, others bigger. They were usually about something completely insignificant, and involved me desperately trying to mediate.

They had different styles. Brit would raise her voice; Flora would plug her ears. They could both give as good as they got. But this fight—I don't even remember how it started—got out of hand. We were in Flora's room, and it was summer. The windows were open and the heat was stifling, no breeze to sway the curtains.

In my memory, I can see her room just the way it was then— a perfect snapshot. The posters of pop stars, the pink-striped bedspread. The mobile over her bed that she made herself—double-sided bits of poster board with line drawings of fairies on them that she had painstakingly colored in. The shelf crammed with stuffed animals—so many it looked ready to tip off the wall under the weight of them, their faces squished next to one another, tucked together like they were posing for a group photo.

A bookshelf stood next to Flora's desk, and on the shelf right at eye level was Flora's prized possession—her miniature greenhouse.

Her dad was serving in Afghanistan at the time. He had spent ages putting the greenhouse together before he left, a gift for Flora's tenth birthday. He had worked on it at a table in the garage, setting plastic bins over the pieces so they wouldn't get swept up or blown away. He rigged up a magnifying glass to make the tiny flowers, cut from colored paper, threaded onto green wire.

When I was really little, I thought that Flora's dad was the biggest man in the world, as tall as a mountain. When I got older, I realized he was actually shorter than my dad—it's just that he was built like a superhero, like one of Terrance and Dash's action figures. I remember marveling at how someone with such bulk and strength could make something so delicate. So detailed and small and intricate.

*To Flora, Love Papa*, it said underneath, scrawled out in marker.

I don't remember what Brit and Flora were arguing about. But there were raised voices and rolled eyes and hands thrown up in the air, and voices raised even louder, and then Brit was turning—this was the stomping-off portion, I knew it—but instead of stomping off, Brit grabbed something from the shelf and hurled it to the ground.

The greenhouse.

Flora let out a cry at the same time I yelled "Don't!" but it was too late. The greenhouse had hit the floor with a sickening crunch, the plastic panels breaking apart instantly, the shelves and tools and plants inside smashing into so many tiny pieces.

We all stood there staring at it for a moment. And then Flora let out a sound, thin and high-pitched, and fell to her knees in front of the broken bits. Her hands hovered over the wreckage before she picked up the tiny orange door and clutched it to her chest, her shoulders beginning to shake with silent sobs.

I looked at Brit, her face stricken. She turned and ran out.

I knelt by Flora and put an arm around her, and she leaned against me.

"It's okay," I told her. "It's okay. We'll glue it back together."

She said something but it came out all garbled amid the tears. All I could make out was *Papa*.

"We'll fix it," I said. "I'll fix it."

I found Brit in her backyard, in the tree with the swoopy branch. I was terrible at tree climbing, and it took me three tries just to get up into it. Even then I couldn't get out onto the swoopy branch, which left me talking to the back of Brit's head.

Except I didn't know where to start. I knew she knew how bad that was.

"Say it," she said after a while, her voice thick. I could count on one hand the number of times I had seen Brit cry.

"Say what?"

"That I'm the worst person in the entire world. I'm a piece of garbage. I shouldn't even exist."

"I don't think that."

She looked back at me, her face red and tear-streaked. Her voice hitched on a sob. "I do."

It was quiet.

"I didn't mean to break it," she choked out finally. "I swear. I just meant to break *something*. Is that the same? Does it make me as bad?"

I didn't speak. I didn't know. The end result was the same, either way.

Brit and I slept over at Teen Zone 2, the night of the Bloomington trip. The Megan Pleasant mission that wasn't about that at all, had never been about it, not even a little bit.

I woke up first the next morning, and stared up at the ceiling until I heard Brit move.

"You lied," I said.

Brit rubbed a hand over her eyes and left it there. "S'too early."

"You lied, Brit." I pulled myself to my feet. It seemed better to have this conversation standing.

"Hate to break it to you, but I lie all the time."

"No, you don't."

"If you really think that, then you think my last statement is true, ergo, I am a liar, ergo, it's too fucking early and I am too fucking depressed to have this conversation."

I thought about what Brit said last night—*How can you know you're a good person if you're never tested? We should all lie more often, just to make sure.*

I stood there for a moment.

"Don't you have work today?" I said.

She snorted, not bothering to lift her head, to even look at me. "I got fired."

I took a deep breath in, let it out.

Then I turned and left.

# thirty-nine

Brit was the last to arrive at band rehearsal on Monday, but she made it all the same, sliding into the empty seat next to Dash.

We got together at break time, Terrance and Dash taking Becca's and Chelsea's empty seats in front of me. I wasn't sure if Brit would join us—I could see her fussing with her drum a bit out of the corner of my eye—but eventually she came over.

They all talked, for a bit, like nothing out of the ordinary had happened this past weekend, like Brit hadn't taken us on a wild-goose chase followed by a catatonic freak-out.

Finally I couldn't take it. "Are we gonna talk about Saturday?" I said, in the middle of Terrance's story about work.

I was looking at Brit, but she was studiously ignoring me.

"What's happening on Saturday?" Terrance said.

"*Last* Saturday."

Brit looked up from her nails. At Terrance, not me. "What were you saying?"

"Brit. Seriously. You lied. To all of us. You said Megan's brother was at the party and he wasn't."

It was quiet for a moment. Then Terrance cleared his throat awkwardly.

"I mean . . . technically not *all* of us, since Flora and I weren't super involved in . . . whatever happened," he said, glancing at Flora.

"Yeah, lucky you," I replied, and Brit looked at me finally, eyes narrowed.

"Megan Pleasant doesn't owe you shit, Sophie. Neither does Acadia, or the band, or me, or August, no one owes you anything. I feel like you don't understand that."

"Let's not do this here," Dash said, voice calm and even.

I shook my head. "It was messed up to track down Tanner like that, it was *dangerous*—"

"Yeah." Brit nodded. "Yeah, maybe it was messed up to go after Tanner. But maybe it was also creepy as fuck to go to a random party just to meet some singer's *brother* to try to convince him to get her to play at our stupid festival. Maybe that's pretty messed up too, if you actually think about it."

"You're always so careless." I blinked hard. "You are."

"It's not my fault you care too much! About everyone! And everything!"

"I would do anything for the people I love."

"Yeah and maybe all one hundred and fifty-two people you love would like you to chill out and worry about your own damn self for like five minutes, Sophie! Maybe we're drowning in your constant need to fix *every little thing*, Jesus Christ, maybe it's suffocating us! And maybe if you stopped for a second and actually worried about yourself, you'd realize that getting Megan to come here isn't gonna change jack shit."

"It'll help us raise the money," I said, trying to keep my voice steady.

"If you think that's what this is about to you, then you're out of your mind."

"Hey." Suddenly Chelsea appeared next to Terrance, holding her flute like a baton. "Just an FYI, everyone else here doesn't feel like hearing about your rando friend-group drama."

"Fucking shut it, Chelsea," Brit snapped without even skipping a beat.

"I don't mind hearing it, to be honest," Becca offered from next to her. "We'll just hear about it from everyone else anyway."

"Whatever." I stared at Brit like I could stare through her. "That's fine. If you want to go around lying and punching people and doing stupid shit, then that's totally your business, isn't it? If you want your life to be one huge unmitigated Coach Junior of a failure, then I should just sit back and fucking let it happen, right?"

Brit looked as though I had slapped her.

No one spoke, not even Chelsea and Becca, who probably wanted their seats back. Ms. Hill had moved back to the front of the room—she was going to start the practice back up—but none of us moved.

It felt like the floor was slipping away, like I couldn't even feel the seat under me.

"All right, folks," Ms. Hill said, and people were moving back to their spots, picking up their instruments.

I stood, cut past Chelsea and Becca, and left.

When I got home, I fell across my bed, pulled out my phone.

I opened a text to Ciara.

*Brit doesn't get to be mad at me, it isn't fair. She says a million shitty things and I say one shitty thing and it's supposed to be equal? Like she gets to be just as hurt as me? It shouldn't work like that, it's bullshit, this whole thing is bullshit, and I wish you were here, you were supposed to come back, I wish you were coming back*

I stared at it, the letters swimming in front of my eyes, and then I deleted it.

I squeezed my eyes shut, clutched the phone to my chest. I almost jumped out of my skin when it buzzed with a message a few moments later.

It was Flora:

*Wanna sleep over tonight?*

I didn't answer. Instead, I tapped open the window for WHERE WILL YOU SPEND ETERNITY. Paused, and then removed myself from the group.

When evening came, I told my parents I was going to Flora's.

I quietly got my bike out of the garage, wheeled it across the grass, crossed around back, and cut through the yard that backed up onto ours.

Then I pedaled away.

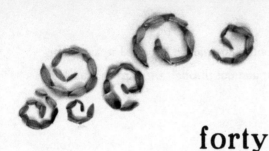

# forty

People were meeting up at Jasmine Mead's tonight. I knew Dash had to work, so Brit wouldn't have a ride if we didn't go together. Flora probably wouldn't go if Brit didn't, and Terrance wouldn't if Flora didn't, and who knew what August thought of anything.

So I went, because I wanted to be with people who weren't my friends.

Not that they weren't my friends—they were. The seniors on the drum line, the girls from the color guard who I sat with in world lit last semester. It just wasn't the same kind of thing, and maybe that was good. Maybe that was less complicated. We could just have fun.

And I did have fun.

I ended up in the living room, dancing with Tegan Wendall and some other girls. I drank, and drank some more—level-three Brit drunkenness maybe, except this wasn't Brit drunkenness at all, this was Sophie drunkenness, which was its own relatively uncharted thing. I didn't know the levels of it.

I didn't know which level was stumbling into the bathroom, looking for my phone to call someone, and realizing I didn't have my phone at all. Not caring.

I didn't know which level was throwing my arms around Tegan Wendall's neck because she was so pretty, really, she genuinely was. Her body was insane, it was absolutely unreasonable, and yet she had this big goofy smile that squished her cheeks up, crinkling her eyes so that they looked almost closed. She could take pictures with a serious expression and look perpetually glamorous if she wanted to, but she always did that big-toothed grin.

Tegan and I danced, and the beat of the song was loud and pounding and it all became a swirl in my mind—*community colleges, state schools, private universities,* and *I saw a mullet today!!!!* and *I talked to mom about the visit* and *Miss you lots.* And I spotted Troy Fowler across the room, laughing unpleasantly just like he had that night in the kitchen with August, the scene of the beer can demonstration, and suddenly all I could think of was the slap of his hands coming together in fourth grade, of the sheets held up around the terrible car crash he saw, *so people couldn't see the dead bodies when they pulled them out.*

Was *dead bodies* redundant? When do people ever refer to it as a body unless it's a dead one? Pop songs, maybe? *Get your body on the dance floor*—that's what I was doing now, but it had to be qualified, the body had to belong to someone. No one sang about "*the* body"—just "*your* body" or "*my* body" and if you were addressing someone about their body or yours, you were both alive, right? Get *the* body on the dance floor was way more sinister. *The* implied emptiness. The body was vacant. No one was home.

Everything was tilting a little.

And loud, too loud, and Tegan was looking at me with concern in her eyes, very far from the squishy-cheeked grin. I wondered how much of the *bodies* discourse I had said out loud.

"Are you okay, Sophie?"

"I'm excellent," I said, but she didn't look like she believed me.

She disappeared after that, and I was sad, because I would have rather she smiled than disappear, but then she returned at some point, parting through the crowd with August behind her.

He looked tired—hair tousled, dark smudges under his eyes—but still undeniably, annoyingly attractive.

He leaned into me, and for a second I thought he was going to kiss me, but instead he put his mouth by my ear, talking over the pound of the music.

"Let's go home, okay?"

# forty-one

August led me out, one of my arms around his neck, one of his around my waist. It was the same way we had taken Brit out to the car, what felt like ages ago at that party at Tegan's.

"You have good shoulders," I told him. For some reason, it seemed pressing for him to know. "You should get a tattoo across your shoulders," I continued. "And then I can lick it off."

A choked laugh escaped him abruptly.

"Jesus." He tightened his grip on me. "Jesus, you're drunk."

"I am. I think I'm very drunk. Maybe that's good. Maybe I'll forget everything. I think it would be awkward next time I see you if I remember that bit about licking your tattoo off."

He didn't speak, just marched us forward.

"You have to forget it too, though," I said as we reached the front door. "You have to promise."

He just looked at me for a moment.

"You have to," I insisted.

"I promise," he replied, eyes strangely solemn. Then he opened the door and led me out to the front, looking up and down the street and then taking out his phone.

"Can't call Dash, he's working," I said. "Can't call Flora, Flora can't drive. Terrance can, but Dash won't let him drive the Cutlass 'cause he backed their mom's car into the mailbox last year." My voice stuck. "Can't call Brit. She hates me. Can't call Ciara." I shook my head. "She didn't want to come back for the summer." Suddenly tears sprang into my eyes, hot and stinging. "We fought, you know. She tried . . . She wanted to . . ."

"It's okay." He squeezed my hand. "It's all right."

Headlights appeared down the street, and suddenly the Cutlass was pulling up. It wasn't Dash, though—Brit hopped out of the driver's side.

"Why haven't you been answering your phone?" she demanded. "Why did you leave the chat?"

I couldn't lose the thread of the conversation. "I wouldn't text her back," I said, and more tears pricked my eyes. "For so long, I went so long—"

"It's all right." August's voice was gentle. "She's here now."

"Not Brit." I shook my head again. Not Brit. I had Brit, even when I didn't. "Ciara."

Brit's face turned sad.

"Here. Come on."

And she was opening the car door and guiding me into the back seat.

"I wouldn't answer her," I said. "For ages."

"It's okay, Sophie," Brit said.

"It's not. It's not okay." I was crying in earnest now.

She cupped my face, wiped her thumbs roughly under my eyes. "You're drunk. It can make the bad things feel worse, if you're not careful."

Brit didn't know what she was talking about—nothing could make this feel worse. Being drunk didn't magnify it—it just gave it a way out.

"What's she talking about?"

I closed my eyes on the drive, every bump making my stomach lurch. Brit must've thought I was asleep, or passed out, because I heard her eventually telling August, softly, the same sort of way I had described the story of Tanner Barnes and Luke, that night on the porch—

"Her sister passed away," she said, and it never sounded any less painful, never ceased to jolt, like a carnival ride turning you upside down and right side up again too fast. It never didn't cut through me. There was always a second where it sounded unbelievable, like a thing that couldn't have actually happened in real life.

"What? When?"

"At the start of our freshman year. She was in a car accident."

"Fuck," August said softly, and I guess Brit and I were both just people who told him things, unbidden, or maybe he was a person you were just compelled to tell stuff to. "I didn't know. She talks about—I thought that . . ."

I blinked once, twice, but they didn't notice me stirring. I could see Brit's hands gripping the steering wheel, her jaw tight.

I squeezed my eyes shut, and a wave of nausea swept through me. I thought of Teen Zone 2.

We didn't call it that back then, the summer before ninth grade—it was just the Cunninghams' pole shed, with a Ping-Pong table in it, and the lawn chairs we pulled in from the porch, the old couch from the side of the road with lumpy throw pillows that we all sewed in home-ec class. The coffee table that Dash and Terrance made with their dad.

I had gone into the house to use the bathroom, and when I came back, I flopped down on the couch next to Flora. My phone sat on the table in front of us, and it buzzed once.

It was a message from Ciara:

*I know. I miss you too. Like so much*

I frowned.

And opened the chat window, where now, above Ciara's newest message, there was text on the right side of the screen. Three bubbles containing my only response for weeks, since the phone call where she told me she wasn't coming back:

*I'll come*

*I'm sorry*

*I'm only mad cause I miss you so much*

I looked up.

Brit and Dash were both holding Ping-Pong paddles, balancing a ball on each. Flora was hugging one of the lumpy pillows, looking at the ceiling. Only Terrance met my eyes.

Little seventh-grade Terrance. The shortest kid in his class, big brown eyes, hair shaved close. He looked closer to ten than thirteen—that's how it was until high school, when he started stretching out, inching up on Dash little by little.

"Who sent this?" I said.

Nobody replied.

"Who sent it?"

Nothing.

"It's none of your business!" I exploded. Brit's paddle dipped, the ball tipping off and bouncing away across the floor. "It's nobody's business, you guys can't just go in my phone and send stuff like it was me!"

"Sophie, listen—" Terrance began.

"That's not okay. How could you think—it's totally messed up! It's totally violating my privacy and my—consent—how could you—" I couldn't even finish. I stormed out.

I was trying to extract my bike from the tangle with Brit's and Flora's bikes on the ground when Terrance approached, alone.

"It was my idea, so don't be mad at everybody," he said. "I typed it out and everything."

I didn't speak, yanking my bike to disengage its pedals from Flora's.

"It's just . . ." His face twisted with concern. "I was just thinking like, if I were you, and it was Dash . . . I just . . ." He shook his head. "I get how you feel, but, like, this isn't helping. You're mad because you don't get to see her, because you miss her so much, so you totally ignore her instead? It makes no sense."

I finally got my bike out. I didn't say anything. Just got on and started to pedal.

"Sophie."

Terrance ran alongside me, passed me before I could amp up speed and stopped in front so I was forced to stick my feet out, grind to a halt. He grabbed the handlebars and looked right at me.

"I know it wasn't right. Technically." He shook his head. "And I'm sorry. But also I'm not."

I backed my bike up, pulling the handlebars from his grasp, and then pedaled away, ignoring him as he called after me.

I was in the back seat of the Cutlass, and then suddenly I wasn't anymore. I found myself at Brit's house, somehow. A series of quick cuts, except they weren't quick at all—a dragging montage of the car and me trying to get my feet under myself, of Brit's arms and August's arms and a pounding nausea that had taken over.

I ended up in Brit's room, curled around her wastepaper basket. She was afraid to set me up in the bathroom, lest her parents wake up in the night, so I puked into plastic grocery bags, which Brit somehow disposed of—I didn't quite track their disappearance.

We had lost August somewhere along the way, maybe once we

got to Brit's room—maybe they had a talk by the door, in hushed tones. Maybe he had helped put me in Brit's bed, before I ended up on the floor, and maybe he had paused for a moment, looking at me, with his hands loosely curled at his sides, something like sorrow etched on his face, except that didn't make any sense.

Now it was just me and Brit. She sat on the floor across from me, her back against the wall.

I threw up until I couldn't anymore, and when I curled up on the floor, she took the trash can away and slipped a pillow under my head and put a blanket over me. I felt both too cold and too hot at the same time. My skin hurt.

"You're being nice to me," I said finally, voice croaky.

"Yeah?"

"Thought you were mad at me."

"Why would I be mad at you? I was the one being an asshole."

It was quiet for a bit. I thought she'd get up, get ready for bed, but she just stretched her legs out, rubbing one socked foot over the other. Finally she spoke.

"Do you remember when we were little, and that girl Ashley was babysitting us, and we were playing hide-and-seek outside and I peed my pants?"

I did remember it, vaguely. Mostly I remember that Brit had cried that day.

"I had to pee so bad, but I was seeking. It got worse and worse but I just kept looking because what if I went inside to go to the bathroom and you thought I gave up? What if you thought I wasn't going to find you? So I kept on looking, and then I peed myself, and I was so embarrassed. But you just drew me pictures of flowers while she cleaned me up, and you were . . . soft toward me, like it wasn't my fault. Like it was something bad that had happened to me, instead of something stupid that I had done."

"It wasn't stupid. You were a little kid. You had to pee."

She didn't speak for a bit after that, and when she finally did, her voice sounded odd. "I just don't want you to ever think that I'm not going to find you. Okay?"

I nodded. "Okay."

# forty-two

I shuffled to the bathroom the next morning. Brit's bed was empty when I woke up, but I could hear someone moving around in the kitchen, so I moved there next, slow and zombielike. Everything was too bright.

It wasn't Brit standing in front of the fridge, though. Luke looked up at me, raised an eyebrow.

"Some night, huh?"

I nodded and instantly regretted the movement.

"Brit went for a run, said she'd be right back. Probably thought you'd sleep longer."

"Nope," I managed. "Awake."

He pulled some stuff out of the fridge. "Want some toast?"

"No." Wasn't going to make the head-shaking mistake again.

"Sure you do." He started untwisting the tie on a loaf of bread.

I thought about that night in Bloomington, about Brit laying into Tanner Barnes. I couldn't imagine she had told Luke about any of it—seeing Tanner, or even the idea of wanting to see Tanner in the first place.

She thought of everything that had happened with Tanner as ruining Luke's life. But Luke was still here, setting down a plate of slightly burnt toast with butter in front of me.

"You gotta eat something," he said kindly, and he was older, and thinner, and a little rougher-looking, but his eyes were the same as those of the boy who used to bike up and down the street with Ciara's hands on his shoulders.

Brit felt like staying in Acadia was a failure somehow. Maybe Luke was stuck. I knew he drank too much sometimes, smoked too much weed, stayed out too late. Argued with their folks. Wanted to move out. Didn't. People talked about his "lost potential," like it was something he'd misplaced, like a glove or an umbrella. But maybe potential was more like a candle—you could relight it. You just had to find a flame.

Maybe he would. Or not. I didn't know.

He filled up a cup with water, set it down next to my plate.

"Go on," he said. "You'll feel better."

I went back to Brit's room after breakfast, laid across her bed, turned to face the window.

At the desk underneath it, newspapers had been laid down, and a number of odds and ends and bits of wood were strewn about, around a small three-sided box. A new miniature kit. Probably for Christmas.

After Flora and Brit's big fight, after the greenhouse was broken, Mrs. Feliciano had called us over the next time she saw Brit and me out in my yard. She took us into her room and pulled a box out from under the bed and opened it—it contained the wreckage of the miniature greenhouse.

"Flora said there was an accident," she said.

Neither of us spoke.

She reached into the box and pulled out a paper pamphlet. "I found the booklet that Papa used to make it." She looked up at both of us, from Brit to me and then back again. "We can put it back together, can't we?"

Brit nodded.

Mrs. Feliciano took us to the table in the garage where Flora's dad had built the greenhouse, showed us the box of tools he used— pliers and scissors and toothpicks and glue. She told us we could use the stuff anytime—she would leave the back door to the garage open.

I would've helped—I wanted to—but Brit took over reconstruction of the greenhouse entirely. By the end of the summer, she had put it back together as best she could. It didn't look exactly the same, but it was whole again, at least.

I wasn't there when she gave it to Flora—just came over one day to find it back on the bookshelf in its original home.

Brit didn't stop there. She asked for a miniature kit for Christmas that year, and by spring, Flora had a tiny bookstore as well, and then an art studio, a dressmaker's shop. We never really talked about the miniatures—beyond complimenting them when Flora showed us—and I got the feeling that Brit didn't want us to, that it was something between her and Flora. Penance, at first, but then something that was unique to them, special between them.

I was still staring at the latest kit on Brit's desk when she got back from her run. She entered the room quietly, saw me awake on the bed.

"Gonna shower," she said, grabbing some clothes out of the dresser. "Make sure you call in at Safeway."

I squeezed my eyes shut. I had forgotten I was supposed to work today.

"Brit," I said as she headed back to the door. She paused. "Thanks for—"

She shook her head. "Don't mention it."

# forty-three

I babysat for Harper that evening.

Part of me wanted to cancel—I felt like the living dead—but I stayed in all day, and managed to get it together by six o' clock.

August wasn't there. I couldn't help but feel relief—I had no idea what to say to him.

Heather and Cadence were at another dance thing. They had left in a flurry, Heather searching for Cadence's ballet shoes while pointing out stuff in the kitchen for Harper. "I got some of those squeezie things she likes, she can have one of those if she's still hungry after dinner," she said, hurriedly pulling on some sandals. "And there's a bunch of stuff in there for you if you want. August made some mac and cheese earlier but didn't eat it, so go to town."

Then they were gone, and it was just me and Harper, who didn't want anything more than food and attention.

It was Kyle who came home first. Harper had fallen asleep in my arms, and I was too tired to get up and put her in her crib. Anyway, it was comforting—the warm weight of her, adjusting every so often, making little grousing sounds.

Kyle took her from me when he arrived, dropping a kiss to the top of her head. But instead of heading to her room, he looked at me.

"Want to see something we've been working on for August?"

"You and Harper?" I said with a small smile.

"Yeah, she's crack with a band saw," he replied, and I flashed on that first night in the kitchen with August—*I saw her change the oil on the car yesterday.*

I stood and followed Kyle into the kitchen, through the door to the basement. Harper slept on, face smooshed against Kyle's shoulder.

Past the laundry area was a door that Kyle pushed through.

There were a few windows set high up into the wall, and carpeting down where there had been bare concrete floor before. Also, actual walls and an actual ceiling. The light was still a bare bulb with a pull cord set into one of the walls—"Gotta get something better for lighting," Kyle said—but it was a real room.

"Just finished painting yesterday. I've got a mattress and box spring coming from one of the girls at work, said they've barely used it. And I was thinking—we were wanting to get a new TV this year anyway—you know how Heather gets with the Black Friday sales—so maybe we could put the old one down here, for gaming or whatever, get a couple of chairs or something, I think there's enough

246

room for it. . . ." He turned to me. "Heather picked the carpet and the paint color and all that. We wanted it to be kind of a surprise . . . his birthday is next month, and we've got to get him out of the kitchen, you know, that was really only a temporary solution, and a pretty terrible one at that, even though he insisted . . ." He trailed off. "What do you think?"

I thought about what August had said—*They're good people. So I'm gonna make it easy on them.*

And on the heels of it, Terrance that day at Teen Zone 2:

*I know it wasn't right. Technically. And I'm sorry. But also I'm not.*

"He's going to leave," I said. "He told me . . . I think he's going to leave soon. I think he thinks it would be better for you guys. If he didn't live here anymore."

Kyle blinked. "What?"

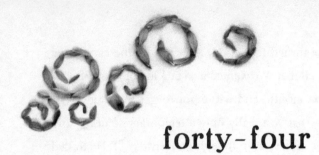

# forty-four

Kyle put Harper in bed, and I was gathering up my stuff when August came through the kitchen door.

Drunkenness, and its aftermath, had not allowed me to forget *You should get a tattoo across your shoulders. And then I can lick it off.* It was the first unmerciful thing that popped into my head on seeing him.

"Hey," August said, and it wasn't an official declaration of joint remembrance, but it wasn't *not* that, either.

And then Kyle's footsteps approached.

August looked past me. "What's up?"

"Is it true? Are you planning to leave?" Kyle's voice was measured, his face neutral.

August's gaze shot back to me, hurt in his eyes. "You told him?"

"Were you going to say anything?" Kyle said, before I could respond. "Give us a warning? Or were you just gonna skip out?"

Silence. August squeezed his eyes shut briefly and then looked toward the ceiling. "I . . . I'm really grateful for everything you've done for me—"

"This is a weird way to show it."

I spoke: "I think maybe August—"

"Don't," August said. "Just . . ." He shook his head.

"I think we probably need to talk this one out just the two of us, Soph," Kyle said evenly, and then pulled his wallet from his back pocket to pay me. "Thanks for watching Harper tonight."

August turned away when I moved past him to get to the back door. I paused in the doorway, looked back at the two of them—August's head hung, Kyle with his arms folded—and then I left.


I couldn't take back the text messages that Terrance had sent that day in Teen Zone 2, the summer before freshman year.

*I'll come*

*I'm sorry*

*I'm only mad cause I miss you so much*

I couldn't tell Ciara that it wasn't me who had finally answered. And I couldn't tell her that it wasn't true, because it was.

By the time I had gotten home that afternoon, thrown my bike down outside, and stomped upstairs, she had sent me another message saying, *Please come visit.*

And so I replied,

249

*Ok.*

Terrance is the reason I saw my sister that summer. We went to the zoo and an art museum. She and Ravi took me out to dinner. We made root beer floats with her roommates, watched our favorite movies. I had the best time. I didn't know it was the last time.

If I knew—if I had known, and I couldn't do anything to stop it—I would've told her I loved her more. I would've told her how I hoped that I could be like her one day, that I could be even half as funny, half as smart, half as kind. I hoped that I would find someone who looked at me the way Ravi looked at her, but even more, I hoped that I would look at someone the way she looked at him. She loved with her whole heart. I wanted to be like that.

I would tell her all those things, if I could, but I wouldn't change anything else about that week, because it was perfect—its only failing in that it had to end.

I opened a text to August that night and began to type out an explanation. Erased it, tried to say it another way, to phrase it better. Erased that too.

In the end, I wrote, *I hope you can forgive me*, and pressed send.

# forty-five

I worked the next day, and it was only on my break that I saw a missed call from Heather.

I called her back, and she picked up on the first ring.

"Hey, I saw that you—" I began.

"Is August with you?"

"No. I'm at work."

"Was he with you last night? Did he stay at your place?"

Something in my stomach seized. "No. What happened?"

She let out a breath. "He and Kyle, last night, I guess they had an argument. I thought everything was okay when we went to bed, but when we woke up, he was gone. His stuff is gone."

*  *  *

"Where would he go?" Dash said, both of us standing outside Safeway. His shift was almost finished, but mine was only halfway through. I didn't care. I left anyway.

"Heather said he didn't take a bike or anything."

"So he couldn't be too far. Unless he hitchhiked."

I sent out a text to everyone. And then I called August, but it rang out. I texted him too:

*Where are you? If you're somewhere close we'll come pick you up*

I amended it:

*Or if you're not*

*We'll pick you up anyway*

Dash tried calling too, to the same result.

*Please answer if you get this*, I added as Dash started up the car.

We drove through town—past school, and the athletic fields, past Fairview Park. Clouds were gathering, the branches of the willows swaying as the wind made patterns in the surface of the pond.

Texts began to roll in:

*I checked at dollar depot, they said he wasn't in today but he was scheduled*, Flora said.

*I'll ask around downtown*, Terrance sent.

*Go to Bygones*, I replied. *Just in case.*

We crossed the railroad tracks, wound through the industrial part of town—the grain elevator, the manufacturing buildings. We circled back and went down Main again, this time turning down 40, through the neighborhood back there. I don't know what I expected to see, but I know what I wanted—August walking down the street, his backpack on. Sitting conveniently on a park bench. Easily spotted, easily convinced to come home.

We were heading out toward the fields when the first raindrops broke through the clouds overhead. A few warning ones, like the first couple of fireworks they send up on the Fourth to signal the start of the show. Then the sky opened up.

My phone buzzed with a message from Brit:

*You should check Megan's house*

I blinked.

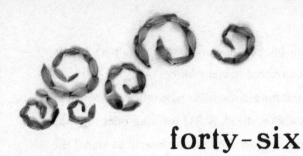

# forty-six

We rolled to a stop in front of the Pleasant place. It had lost all appeal to me since the Bloomington trip. I could hear Brit's voice at band practice—*Maybe that's pretty messed up too, if you actually think about it.*

The rain was coming down heavy, water streaming in sheets through gaps in the roof of the front porch. Dash shut off the car and we ran around to the back, shoving the piece of plywood aside and ducking in.

It was hard to see inside, with how dark it had gotten outside. Dash pulled out his phone and it cast a pale white light, illuminating the probably kitchen of Megan Pleasant's almost-house.

The pound of rain was loud. We were both soaked through, our forest-green Safeway polo shirts turned dark.

I moved through the kitchen, peering down the hall of the new addition.

"Look," Dash said suddenly, and shone the light toward a backpack sitting on the ground in the wide doorway leading to the old side of the house.

"August?" I called, moving back that way.

A muffled shout sounded in response, but I couldn't tell where it was coming from.

I spun around. "August?"

"Sophie?"

I stepped into the old part of the house, and with the relatively little light coming in through the windows, I could see an irregular patch at the center of the floor that was darker than the rest of it.

I moved toward it immediately, and heard a strangled "DON'T" from below, followed by an incredible string of expletives. I froze.

"Don't move!" August yelled. "Don't come closer. It's not stable." Another run of curses, which ended, "God, I'm glad you're here." There was a desperate edge to his voice, like he was on the brink of bursting into laughter or tears. Or both.

"Are you hurt?" Dash called.

"Dash?"

"Yeah."

"Stay back. And yes. Yeah. Will you call Kyle?"

I pulled up Kyle on my phone and threw it to Dash. Then I got on the floor, lying down on my stomach.

"What are you doing?" Dash said.

"Call him." I inched forward, slowly, the way you'd approach a break in the ice of a frozen pond. I didn't go to the very edge of the break in the floor, but close enough that I could see through a narrow gap between two of the broken-off floorboards.

It was dark down there, but I could just make out August's form, lying below.

"Can you move?"

"Get back," he said, voice hoarse. "It's not safe."

"Can you move?" I repeated. "Wiggle your fingers and toes?"

"Yes," he bit out. "But I can't get up. My leg . . ."

"Do you see stairs? Some way we can get down there?"

There had to be an entrance from outside. I could hear Dash on the phone, but I could hardly pay attention to what he was saying. I felt electrified, awash in how incredibly, monumentally stupid it was to have ever come here at all, and the knowledge that August never would've even known about this place if it weren't for me. It was all I could do to keep my voice steady, to sound as though my heart wasn't trying to escape my chest.

"August," I prompted, when he didn't reply.

"Not that I can see."

Dash stayed in the doorway between the old house and the addition. "Kyle's on his way," he said. "They've called EMS."

"Good. They're coming," I told August.

"Keep him talking," Dash said.

"Can you see anything else down there?"

"Like what, an elevator?" August replied, and the tiniest bit of relief trickled through me, because if he could still be a smart-ass, he was probably at least a little bit okay.

"Yeah, any elevators?"

"No." A pause. "But there might be raccoons. I hear rustling."

"Don't think about them."

"They've got tiny thumbs. They could rip my face off."

"I'll fight them if they try."

He huffed a laugh, which turned into a hiss of pain.

"You okay?"

"Hurts."

I glanced up at Dash, who said, "They're coming," again, like he knew I needed to hear it.

"Will you guys do something for me?" August asked.

"Yeah."

"Sing Terrance's song about the boots?"

I let out a breath. "I can't think of a more inappropriate time for that song."

"Yeah, that's exactly why we have to sing it," Dash said, smiling the slightest bit.

So we did, pausing line by line to quiz August on what might come next. He had only heard it twice, back at that first party at Tegan's house, but he had absorbed the lyrics surprisingly well. Maybe Terrance really was a good songwriter—catchiness is a definite asset.

We got to the chorus ("And I just do love you / and those boots that are bluuuuuuue") when the slam of a car door sounded from outside.

# forty-seven

Kyle made us go outside while the firefighters worked to get August out of the basement. I didn't want to leave, but Kyle's expression brooked no argument, so Dash and I waited in the Cutlass. It was still raining, but not quite as hard as before.

Eventually they wheeled August out on a stretcher. He was covered in dust and dirt, and held one arm against himself. His face was gray, his expression pinched.

Dash and I jumped out of the car.

"We'll take him to Saint Anthony's," one of the EMS guys was saying to Kyle.

"That sounds expensive," August said tightly. "I'm fine. I can walk it off."

"You're seriously making jokes right now?" Kyle's expression was a complex mix of relieved and exasperated. I could tell because I felt exactly the same way.

"Didn't break my funny bone," August replied, and managed a smile.

Dash offered to follow Kyle to Saint Anthony's. Kyle just shook his head, said we should both go home and get some rest, that we had done a great job.

I didn't want to go home, though. I wanted to go where August was going, and luckily Kyle seemed to understand that.

So he and I drove to Saint Anthony's together, thirty minutes of Kyle nervously drumming his fingers against the steering wheel.

When we arrived at the ER, a nurse took us back to a room full of monitors and machines. August wasn't there. The nurse told us he was headed for some X-rays, that we could wait here for him.

I couldn't sit. Just moved back and forth, looking at the different machines. There was a tightness in my chest that only eased slightly when they wheeled August back in.

The ultimate diagnosis was a broken ankle, bruised ribs, a sprained wrist.

"One in every flavor," August said with a weak smile.

"You're like the Yum Yum Shoppe of bodily harm."

He shook his head. "Fourteen flavors of fun. I would need eleven more injuries."

"You'll probably have a bunch of bruises."

"Eleven of them?"

"Yup."

"Then I'm the Yum Yum Shoppe."

I went outside eventually to call my mom. I had texted on the drive here, but it wasn't the same as hearing her voice on the other end of the line, calm and reassuring.

I had about fifty texts from WWYSE. Dash had told everyone what happened. I sent off a quick message and then sat down on the curb. Dropped my head, breathed in deep and let it out slow.

I sat with August while Kyle went out to call Heather with an update.

We were in a room off the center of the emergency department, glass windows lining one side so we could see the nurses at the station in the middle, see Kyle pausing to talk to the nurse who had shown us in earlier.

August had an IV taped to the back of his hand, a plastic sensor attached to one of his fingers. He tapped it absently against the bedsheets, looking out in Kyle's direction.

"I couldn't explain it to him right," he murmured.

"Hm?"

"Last night. I couldn't make him understand. So I thought it would be better just to leave now. Get it over with." He shook his head. "But now I've made it so much worse when all I wanted was for—all I wanted to do was not be a burden on them—"

"It's going to be okay," I said.

"She stole," he replied.

"Sorry?"

"My mom. She stole money from her job." A slow blink. "A lot.

260

Over . . . years." He swallowed. "If you don't steal that much . . . and if you pay it back . . . you might not even have to go to jail. But she just . . . it was too much, for too long. We couldn't pay it back. Sold everything we could but there was just . . . no way."

I didn't speak.

"She told them she did it 'cause she wanted us to have a better life. But that's not . . . you can't shortcut your way to one, can you? It doesn't work like that." A beat. "I always had everything I wanted. Fucking . . . video games and sneakers and shit, I never thought about . . . I never thought. I just lived my life and maybe if I'd . . ." His eyes went liquid. "I never questioned anything. I was selfish. And I didn't learn anything at all, I just kept on being selfish. With everything. Especially with you." He shook his head. "I'm sorry, Soph. I should never have come here in the first place. Shouldn't have made friends, shouldn't have gotten involved—"

"It's not selfish to want people in your life who care about you."

His mouth twisted. "I won't let myself be anyone's responsibility ever again. That's the only way to be sure. That you're not making things worse for everyone you love."

It was quiet.

"Sounds lonely," I said.

He looked up at me, eyes shiny. "But safe."

I shifted my gaze to the IV stand next to August's bed, followed the path of the clear tubing. When I spoke, it was carefully. I wanted to get this right.

"It hasn't done you super well so far, has it? You're on your own for like half a day and you fall into a basement." A pause. "I mean, as far as metaphors from the universe go, it's pretty heavy-handed."

His lips twitched.

"I don't know a whole lot about . . . anything," I said, "but I feel like in general . . . it's probably okay to need people. And to let yourself be needed by them too." I swallowed. "It's not just one-sided, you know. After Ciara—" I shook my head. "After my sister's accident, I started babysitting Cadence. Every Tuesday. They had just moved in. Heather needed a babysitter, and I needed . . . something to help me get through to the next week. It worked both ways."

He blinked, moisture gathering at the corners of his eyes. "I'm glad they were there for you."

"So am I," I said. "They're here for you too."

He shook his head. "Nobody needs me, though."

"Cady needs someone to order pizza in funny voices. She needs someone worthy of the pink bunny quilt, which she obviously thinks you are. Harper needs someone who will look every time she points at something. They both need someone who can read to them in . . . the worst Scottish accent imaginable."

He smiled the faintest bit.

"You help Heather out. You make her laugh. And Kyle . . ." I looked away, swallowed. "I think he's probably really happy for the chance to know his brother."

It was quiet. August looked toward one of the machines, marking his heartbeats with gentle beeps.

"It sounds good when you say it like that," he said eventually.

"So let it be good."

He was about to speak when Kyle reappeared, followed by a doctor and a nurse. They checked August out again, gave him some more medication after he numbered his level of pain, said they would be back to check in again in a little bit.

"And then we can see about getting you discharged," the doctor said.

Kyle's phone buzzed when they left.

"It's Heather again," he said. "I'm gonna—" I nodded, and he stepped out.

It was quiet for a bit, until August murmured: "I feel weird."

"You look weird," I replied automatically, and he smiled, a bit wobbly.

"You're funny."

"That was pretty elementary stuff."

"No, you are." He swallowed. "That's what I like about you. One of the things. There's lots of things."

"You can tell them all to me sometime."

"Would you let me?"

"Yes."

He blinked once, twice. "I think they gave me the good stuff, Soph. I feel weird."

"That's okay. Just enjoy it."

He smiled a little, shut his eyes. Extended the palm of his hand toward me, and I took it.

# forty-eight

We left the hospital late that night—past midnight. The rain had lightened to a drizzle, but the roads were slick, each set of passing headlights casting a glow.

August fell asleep on the drive, propped up carefully in the back seat. His ankle and wrist were splinted, his arm hung in a sling. He would have to go back to the hospital in a few days to meet with an orthopedic doctor and get a hard cast put on his ankle.

Kyle was quiet as we drove. I had never seen him look so tired.

"I'm sorry," I said after a while. There had been so much waiting around at the hospital, but I hadn't said it to him, hadn't been able to make myself say it. Maybe I was a coward, because it was easiest when Kyle couldn't look over at me, when he had to keep his eyes on the road. "I took August to Megan's house the first time.

I showed him how to get in. We should never have gone there."
What if it had happened then? What if Brit had fallen through too?
What if we all had? "It was really stupid."

"It was." He nodded. "But I'm just glad everyone's okay."

His gaze darted to the rearview mirror, then back to the road,
and for a little while the swipe of the windshield wipers was the
only sound.

"I got in an accident when I was in high school," Kyle said eventually. "We were driving out in one of the fields and flipped the
truck. I was banged up, but nothing too bad. I'd never seen my dad
that mad, though. I thought . . . at the time I thought it was because
of the car, but I get it now. How scared he must've been." A pause.
"I didn't know, before having the girls, but it's like a piece of you
exists outside of yourself. It's the most amazing thing, but also, just
like . . . terrifying." He adjusted his grip on the steering wheel. "I
know I'm not, like, his parent, I know that, but . . ." He shook his
head. "Growing up, I knew my dad would do anything for me. Felt
like he always had my back, like he could literally fix anything. I'm
not saying I can be that for August, that I even know how. But he
should have . . . as close to that as I can be. He deserves that."

I thought about the drive home from the party. I could hear
Brit's voice, talking to August as she drove. Telling him about
Ciara.

I looked into the back seat now and wondered if there was any
chance that August was awake. That he could hear what Kyle was
saying.

But August's face was relaxed in sleep.

"You should tell him," I said, and then shook my head, because I could say it better: "I know you don't owe me anything, but will you tell him? Please?"

"We owe you a lot, Soph," Kyle replied. "And yeah. I will."

The house was all lit up when we arrived, the front door open so we could see a rectangle of living room through the storm door, Heather moving inside.

Flora burst out of her house when we pulled into the Conlins' driveway, Brit close behind.

Heather came out too, holding Harper, who was crying. Cady followed, standing on the front stoop, despite Heather's instructions to stay inside.

Flora ran and hugged me, and Brit hovered behind, her arms folded, her mouth in a tense line.

"Is he okay?"

Kyle opened the car door and gently shook August's shoulder. "Buddy?"

August blinked blearily.

"Hey, we're home."

He nodded. "Where's Soph?"

"Here," I said, my voice sticking in my throat.

Kyle and Brit helped him out of the car and into the house, navigating into the living room and settling August on the couch.

"No one would go to bed," Heather told me, bouncing Harper

up and down while she wailed. "Everyone wanted to see Uncle August and no one wanted to sleep."

Cadence's face was full of worry. She stood at Heather's side, clutching a sheaf of construction paper. "We drew you pictures," she said, when August was situated.

"Thanks, Cady." He took them with a lopsided smile, laid them on his lap, and leafed through them one-handed. "These are great."

"I think it's way past bedtime," Heather said, shifting Harper around.

"Will you read to me?" Cadence asked August.

"I will," I said, holding out a hand toward her. "August needs to go to bed too."

Cadence looked up at me, brown eyes big and tired.

"Come on." I wiggled my fingers. "We can read a chapter of *Pooh*."

She nodded, took my hand, and we went inside. She settled against me, and it was only a couple of pages before she fell asleep.

Heather came in with Harper, now sleeping too, and laid her down in her crib.

Brit and Flora were gone when we emerged. August was asleep on the couch, his brow smooth, his mouth parted slightly. All the worry was smoothed from his brow. He looked like a fairy-tale prince you could awaken with a kiss, breaking some centuries-old spell. My fingers itched to smooth his hair back.

I didn't. Just stood in the doorway for a moment, before Heather came up and drew me into a long hug.

"Thank you," she said, slightly muffled. "I thought Cady would never sleep." She gave me a squeeze and then pulled away. "Also, thanks for the other thing." She looked at August. "The main thing."

I smiled a little. "No problem."

# forty-nine

We all went to the Conlins', late the next afternoon. I wasn't sure how up for hanging out August would be, but he had texted: *Everyone should come over*, so we all went.

August thanked us for saving his life. Dash shifted back and forth, looking uncomfortable, but Terrance smiled dazzlingly.

"Anytime. My pleasure. Always here for a lifesaving moment."

"You didn't even do anything!" Brit said.

"Don't underestimate moral support," he answered loftily.

"I mean it," August said, meeting my eyes. "I'd probably still be down there. If it weren't for you."

I glanced away. "Brit was the one who said to look there."

"No, I wasn't," she replied. "Why would I want to save him? Dash's car only seats five."

"Thank you. Seriously," August said.

Brit looked flustered by the sincerity. "Yeah, okay, no big deal. You don't have to throw a parade or anything."

"You do," Terrance said. "And I expect to be grand marshal."

Eventually, we ended up sitting in the backyard, watching Dash and Brit throw a ball for Shepherd.

"I always wanted a dog," Flora said as Shepherd bound happily back to them, the tennis ball in his jaws. "I asked my parents for one when I was little, but they got me a stuffed one instead."

"Stuffed like plush or stuffed like taxidermy?" August asked, and Terrance snorted.

"How amazing would that be? Hey, little Flora, Merry Christmas, here's a dog corpse that we preserved for you. Enjoy!"

"You'd never have to walk it," I offered.

"Stuffed like plush," Flora said. "Obviously."

"I had a stuffed dog when I was little too," August said. "It was my favorite."

"What was its name?"

"I don't remember."

"August," Flora wheedled.

He let out a sigh, and then, begrudgingly: "Auggie-doggie."

"I'm sorry, what?" Brit said as she pried the ball away from Shepherd.

"I was little!"

"What happened to Auggie-doggie?" Flora asked.

"I don't know. Got lost somewhere, I guess."

It was quiet for a bit, just Shepherd's happy panting and Brit's encouragement as he went back and forth for the ball—"The best dog there ever was! The smartest! The squishiest!"

"I had a teddy bear, you know," Terrance said eventually.

"Yeah?"

"Yeah. His name was . . . Terrance-bearance."

"I will fight you," August said.

"I'm dead serious right now."

"Wait, really?"

That thousand-watt grin took Terrance's face. "Of course not."

Brit's bark of a laugh sounded out over Flora's giggles and Dash's low rumble.

"I'll fight all of you!" August roared, but he was grinning too.

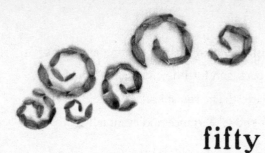

# fifty

I called August as I walked home from work a few days later. He had been back to Saint Anthony's that morning to have a cast put on his ankle.

"Are you home?" I asked.

"I'm at Terrance and Dash's house," he replied, and then there was a rustling.

"Hi, Sophie," Terrance called, slightly muffled.

"How was work?" August said.

"Good. How's the cast?"

"Pretty good. Cady started decorating already. She's got big plans."

"Oh yeah?"

"Yeah, a major art installation. I think once she's run out of cast, she's just going to keep going. I'm going to be fully decorated."

"She's good at it. She colors in Kyle's tattoo all the time." He had a big one on his forearm. "That weird elk thing?"

"Oh yeah. And the playing card."

"Hm?"

"On his back? Ace of hearts. Said he liked it 'cause aces could be high or low, and that's how love could be." A pause. "He also said he was super drunk when he got it."

I stopped short.

I didn't go home after work. I went straight to the Conlins' back door and knocked.

Heather and Kyle were in the kitchen, Kyle sitting at the little table, Heather standing with her back against the sink, both with plates of pie. Heather waved to me through the screen door, gestured me inside.

"Hey, Soph." She set her dish down on the counter. "Want pie?"

"You knew her," I said.

They both just blinked at me.

"Yes, of course I want pie," I added, and sat down at the table across from Kyle.

"Sorry, what's up?" Heather turned to scoop up a piece out of an aluminum pie tin.

"You knew Megan Pleasant," I said, looking at Kyle. "'You're my ace of hearts'? From 'Always You'? She wrote it about you. She was in love with you."

He looked at me a moment. Then he looked down at his plate,

dividing the bit of crust in half with his fork. "She wasn't." He didn't look even the slightest bit surprised, which made me feel all the more vindicated.

"But those songs were about you."

Kyle shook his head. "I didn't say they weren't."

"Then she was in love with you."

"No."

"How do you know? I won't—like, I won't tell anyone, if it's some big secret. I swear."

Heather had turned around at the sink and switched on the faucet. She stood there for a moment, the tap running, and then she looked back at Kyle and nodded.

"I know because she didn't write that song," he said.

"What?"

He smiled a little, chagrined. "She didn't write any of them."

"Not true," Heather said.

"None of the good ones, at least."

Heather shook her head. "Not fair."

I looked at her. "What do you mean?"

She sighed. She looked tired, suddenly.

"I guess that . . . basically"—a shrug—"I'm Megan Pleasant."

# fifty-one

"Wait, what?"

"Not like . . . I mean Megan is Megan, yeah. This isn't like a Hannah Montana scenario. We are two distinct people. But. I wrote her songs," Heather said. "Some of them."

"A lot of them," Kyle clarified.

"'Gave You My Heartland'?"

She nodded. "Everything on the first album. Most of *Letters Home*."

"After that?"

She shook her head.

"How?" I said.

Heather took a deep breath, and then began to talk.

* * *

"It was just a goof at first. All these songs we wrote freshman year of high school—Megan taking them to these producers in Nashville and these guys actually doing something with them. When they finished recording the album, she came back to town for the summer, and we just started up again. We had no idea how the first album would sell, and by the time it came out . . . she was in and out of school, I rarely saw her, but we had written all these songs in the meantime. Those became *Letters Home*. The producers changed some of them up a little, but . . . most of them started as ours."

"Yours," Kyle said.

"She didn't actually grow up here, you know—her folks moved here when she was in seventh grade. But we became best friends. She always talked about singing, about becoming famous. I never . . . I can't sing at all. But I liked to write. I mean, I think every kid has written some shitty lyrics or poems at some point. But to me . . . it was more than that, like I really genuinely liked it. So we would sit around her room and just . . . make stuff up." She smiled a little, wistful, like she was transported back to that room with Megan.

"'Gave You My Heartland' started out as a joke . . . if you brought someone back to Acadia—like maybe you went away to school or wherever and met someone—how would you introduce them to the town . . . and then it just spun out from there."

I shook my head. "But why . . ." Everything I had read.

*Singer-songwriter Megan Pleasant. The pen connected from her heart to the page.* "Why didn't you ever get credit?"

Heather looked away.

"It was . . . we were just kids, at first. I didn't understand what it would become, so I didn't try to make it into a thing." A pause. "She didn't end up finishing school with us. Recording and promo and all that, it became too much. She was traveling more and more. A few years later, after the second album . . . she came back. They were building that house . . . she was in the middle of a tour, but she was playing in Indianapolis, had a day off between shows. Early on, she would invite me out, any time she played close by, but I heard from her less and less . . . I knew how busy she was. But she showed up at Darby Court, where we were living at the time. Cadence was really little then.

"She seemed . . . distracted. She came and sat in the living room and she took out a checkbook. Said she'd pay me right then and there, for everything, so long as I never told another person that I had written those songs. Said she was turning over a new leaf or whatever . . . starting a new chapter in her career. That we wouldn't write anything else together, and that was . . . fine, I guess, it wasn't like . . . I wasn't setting out to be some big songwriter, like she had become this big musician. But really, I think . . . she knew that things might change between us. That she was getting successful, so she thought I would come along asking for money, or—or blackmailing her or some shit." She shook her head. "It was never about the money for me."

"Even though she was getting famous? And rich?"

"We wrote those songs when we were kids. For fun. I never thought of it like that."

"You're a better person than most," Kyle said. "Because she should've fucking paid you from the start, even if you didn't care about credit."

"She was my best friend," Heather said simply. "I loved her. I would've done anything for her."

"So she offered you money?"

"She did. And I was . . . I was insulted, I guess. Not at the money itself—God knows we could've used it—but at the thought that I would betray her like that. That I would . . . sell her out on the internet or whatever, just for some notoriety. And also, I guess . . . I was hurt that . . . it felt like she was cutting me out. It felt . . . final, like in terms of our friendship. She didn't even ask about Cadence, you know. Didn't even want to see her." Heather shook her head. "So I got mad. We fought. She left, and . . . we never talked again. The third album came out, and it was . . ." A shrug. "She was doing what she wanted, finally. I guess. And it worked out for her." There was something final in the way she said it—this was the end of the story. "I'm happy for her."

I told August the whole thing on the phone that night. They never actually swore me to secrecy, but I didn't think it would apply to August, even if they had.

I didn't know what to think. How to feel. Megan wasn't exactly who I thought she was. Neither was Heather. I had to renegotiate both of them in my mind.

At least it prepared me—slightly—for a few nights later, when there was a knock at the door when I was babysitting Harper and Cadence.

And there, on the doorstep, was Megan Pleasant.

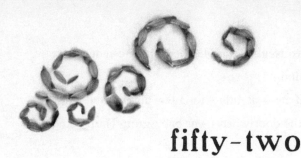

# fifty-two

I don't know why—maybe TV and movies—but I thought famous people always had entourages. Like she should be standing there with a driver and a security guard and a manager and her makeup artist/stylist/best friend who would be holding a palette out, brushing a bit of highlighter onto her cheeks. There should be a reality-TV film crew—two cameras and a sound guy holding a boom or something.

But Megan Pleasant stood on the Conlins' front steps all alone, in a pair of ripped jeans and a faded T-shirt, a leather bag slung over one shoulder. Her hair was as long and shiny as it had been the day I met her, and she was undeniably beautiful—dark lashes, Cupid's bow lips. Alongside the initial shock, I was instantly seized with that feeling—I wanted to be her, but I also wanted her to be *My Girl*—and for a moment I just stood there, frozen.

Was it—could it be possible? The social media outreach had worked? Megan had gotten one or some or all of my messages, and now she was here somehow, she had found me here at the Conlins' house to tell me that, yes, she would play at the fall festival—

"Hi," she said. "Is Heather here?"

*IT'S ME, SOPHIE, FROM THE EMAILS*, my brain yelled.

"Uhhh . . ." I said out loud.

"Sorry to just show up like this, I know it's late . . . if she's not here, I can come back . . ."

"Uhhh . . ." Just as eloquent.

It was then Shepherd got up abruptly and bounded to the back door, and I heard it swing open, the sounds of conversation between August and Heather filtering in. I looked toward the kitchen, and when I looked back I half expected Megan Pleasant to have vanished, a figment of my imagination.

But she was still there.

"I should've called," she said.

My brain was short-circuiting. Instead of calling out for Heather, I yelled "Megan Pleasant!" in a high and strangled voice, and on the front stoop, actual Megan Pleasant physically recoiled.

"What's up? Why do you sound unhinged?" Heather said, poking her head through the door. Then she froze.

"Hey," Megan said.

Heather blinked. "Hi."

August appeared beside her on his crutches. "Hey, Soph—" Then his eyes grew wide. "Holy shit. The ritual worked."

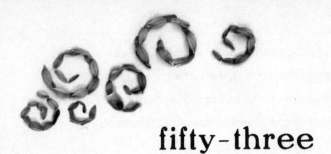

# fifty-three

August and I sat on the window seat in the kitchen with the back door ajar. We could hear Heather and Megan through the screen door.

It started with awkward small talk. Megan said the house was nice. Heather said they'd been there for three years now. Megan asked about her little girl—"Katie?"—and Heather told her about Cadence and Harper. Both snuggled up in bed, both unaware that Acadia's most famous export was sitting on their back patio, next to Cadence's pink Power Wheels Jeep.

Eventually it grew silent.

"Do you want a drink or something?" Heather said. "I could make coffee."

"I'm here to apologize," Megan said.

"My entire career felt fake," she began. "At first . . . you know, it was a whirlwind, of course it was. Being on TV and people knowing my name, doing shows and stuff, it was . . . an absolute dream. I didn't really think about it, what it would become, what *I* would become, using the stuff we had written. Pretending—not pretending, okay—but . . . never admitting that there was someone else involved. Is that the same as pretending?"

I thought of Brit and the greenhouse—*I didn't mean to break it. I just meant to break* something.

Heather didn't respond.

"Everybody praised me for, like . . . my authenticity or whatever. But it wasn't me who was authentic. It wasn't me who loved Acadia and the boy next door and all that. It was you.

"I didn't even know what it was I wanted after a while. What *I* sounded like. I didn't know how to sing something that you hadn't touched. We started working on the third album and they were putting me in the studio, having me meet with producers and talk about my *sound* and the landscape of my career and all that, and I just . . . I wanted to be who I was. I wanted to figure it out, at least, but how could I tell them now that I hadn't known it all along?

"I know it's no excuse, but I just . . . I needed a clean break. I needed to start over. And it felt like . . . to me, it felt like the only thing I could do was try to cut you out. It was shitty from the start, Heather, I know that. I know it. You should've been credited on everything. Forget that we were kids. Fuck it, I should've said it from the beginning, I should've insisted.

"So last time, when I came back . . . I thought I was making it right, but I also . . . it was selfish, I know that, but everything just seemed like . . . like it had gone on for so long, I didn't know if I could ever get out from under it. And it seemed like the only thing to do would be to cut ties, you know?"

Silence.

And then a cry came from Cadence and Harper's room.

"Lemme check on her." There was the sound of a chair scraping against concrete.

"Kiss me," I said, and reached for August. He hesitated for just a second, before pressing his lips against mine.

Heather paused in the doorway, eyebrows raised as we quickly broke apart.

"Subtle."

"We were just—"

"I know what you were just."

"I'll, uh, walk Sophie out," August said.

"Yeah, right. And do that thing where you pretend to say bye and shut the door and then sneak Sophie downstairs? If you're gonna fool around, just go fool around. But—BUT"—she held a finger up to August and me in turn—"use your brain. Both of you. And not the little brains. The big brains."

"Both my brains are big," August said solemnly.

"I swear to God, you are just like your brother sometimes, it's terrifying." She nudged August gently toward the basement door. "Go."

We went. August had to go down the stairs on his butt, but he was pretty quick at it. I carried his crutches down, handed them to him at the bottom of the stairs.

He led me through the door to his new room. It had changed a little since Kyle had shown me—now a mattress and box spring were pushed up underneath the little window on the far wall, and a set of shelves sat against the opposite wall, the contents of August's window atop it. The pink-and-white quilt was among the blankets twisted up on the bed.

Overhead I could hear Heather moving around—footsteps back and forth, like she was bouncing Harper.

"If we crack the window, we should be able to hear," August said, leaning over the side of the bed to reach the small window.

"No, don't."

He paused, eyeing me questioningly.

"I mean. I think we heard enough. It's between them."

"You mean now that we've heard all the good stuff?"

"No." I looked away sheepishly. "Well. Maybe a little. But it's personal. We should . . . leave it to them."

"Then why'd we come down here?"

The kiss upstairs was meant to be a diversion. And our first ones were for research, and our second ones were a mistake. I couldn't keep up. What if all our kisses were like that? What if we just went on kissing for oddball reasons, like because a Kiss Cam is pointed at us at a sporting event, or to generate warmth when we're snowed in with no power—what if we just trope-kissed for the rest of our lives?

"Wanted to see your room," I said after a moment.

"What do you think?"

"It's no kitchen window. But it's pretty nice."

A smile flickered across his face, and then it was quiet.

"Look, Soph—" He paused, dropped his gaze to the ground, took a deep breath. "I know I've messed everything up between us. And I'm sorry, I'm so—"

"I'm still mad at you."

He nodded. "That's fair."

"You left here without leaving a note."

He looked up, eyes shining. "I could leave you one now."

"Yeah?"

"Yeah." He cleared his throat. "Dear Sophie. I will be staying in Acadia for the foreseeable future. I regret to inform you that you're stuck with me." He swallowed. "And that I love you."

It was quiet.

"You didn't sign it," I said. "Where are my fondest wishes?"

August smiled, tentatively. "Fondest—"

I was already kissing him.

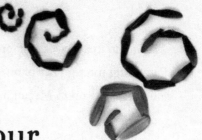

# fifty-four

I lost track of what was happening upstairs, couldn't tell when Heather went back outside, but eventually two sets of footsteps were moving across the length of the ceiling.

We broke apart, August blinking at me. "Is she leaving?"

I sat up. "I have to—" I climbed out of bed, slipped on my shoes. "Sorry, I have to talk to her. Just—quick, I'll be back—"

And I dashed upstairs.

Heather was in the living room when I got up there, shutting the door.

"Is she—"

"Hurry," she said, swinging the door back open.

"Megan!" I called out the front. She was at the end of the drive-way. A large black SUV was parked across the street. A woman was sitting in the driver's seat, probably Megan's age or a little younger, scrolling through her phone, looking bored.

I caught up to Megan, my flip-flops slapping against the front path.

"Sorry," I said when I reached her. She looked a little bewildered, like she had when I originally answered the door. "I just wanted to . . ."

It felt stupid, in person. It felt like asking so much, but somehow at the same time, embarrassingly little? But I had to. I owed it to the band. I took a deep breath and it came out fast:

"The Marching Pride of Acadia is going to the Rose Parade this year and we were wondering if you would be willing to appear at the fall festival this year as part of a fundraising concert?"

"Uh." A wrinkle appeared between her brows. "Uh, yeah, I saw—I read something about that. My publicist showed me a . . . Let me . . . I'll give you my manager's info, you can contact her about it."

I didn't have my phone, or pen and paper, but I could run back inside, I'd be right back—

"I'll text Heather, how about that?" she said, crossing around to the passenger's side of the SUV. The woman in the driver's seat looked up, set her phone aside.

"That would be great. Thank you. Thank you so much."

She nodded, and got into the car.

August and Heather were sitting in the living room when I went back into the house. The TV was on, playing softly.

I sank down on the couch next to August, and we all pretended to watch whatever show this was for a few moments. At least, I was pretending. I was waiting for Heather to say something—anything—but she just sat looking at the screen, expression unreadable.

I wanted to hold August's hand, but I felt embarrassed in front of Heather. Which was silly, seeing as she had sent us downstairs with full knowledge of what would probably happen down there.

"Why'd she come back now?" August asked finally.

"They told her someone got hurt at her house," Heather said. "She got into Springfield a day early for the state fair, thought she'd come out and have kind of a last look at the place, I guess. Said they'll probably knock the house down, try to sell the land."

"Did you tell her it was me?" August said.

"I kept that part to myself," she replied with a wry smile.

It was quiet, until I looked over at Heather. "She said she'd text you her publicist's info, so we can arrange the fall festival stuff."

Heather nodded. "I'll let you know if I hear from her."

What Heather didn't tell us then, and August told me later, was that Megan had brought Heather a huge check. Bigger than last time. She offered her the land as well, the house if she wanted it.

"What would I want with that house?" Heather had told August and Kyle. "We'd have to fix the August-shaped hole in the floor."

She didn't rip up the check, though. She put it in one of the kitchen cabinets. August said he could hear footsteps going in and out of the kitchen all night.

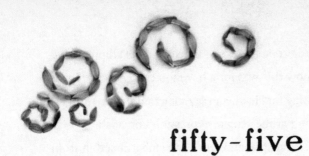

# fifty-five

"I think she probably won't come back," I said on one of our drives after work, Dash behind the wheel. We had demolished some sandwiches from the deli section. I had half a bottle of soda left, but I was more preoccupied with twisting and untwisting the cap than I was with drinking. "Megan. I think she's probably not going to do the show."

I had checked in with Heather a few times, but she hadn't heard anything from Megan. She didn't seem too surprised.

"I really thought I could do it." I fumbled with the cap. "Maybe that's my problem."

"What?"

"That I think I can make something happen just by wanting it enough. Objectively, it's like . . . pretty stupid and naive." August didn't want his mom to go to prison but that didn't keep it from happening. Brit wanted to beat Tanner Barnes but it didn't make her feel any better.

"Maybe," Dash said. "But it's also kind of good, don't you think?"

"Why?"

"It's probably better than thinking that nothing you feel or do can ever make a difference, right? I'd rather believe in something."

"I guess."

It was quiet for a bit, until:

"That's why I didn't tell Brit," Dash said.

"Tell her what?"

He adjusted his grip on the steering wheel. "That whole thing with Tanner."

He didn't go on, but I knew he would, so I didn't prompt him.

"Luke wasn't drugged," Dash said eventually. "It wasn't something done to him. He took that shit on purpose, with Tanner and the rest of them."

"How do you know?" I straightened up in my seat, looked over at Dash even though I knew he wouldn't take his eyes off the road to look back. "The other guys on the team—they would lie. They'd make stuff up to make sure they don't get in trouble."

"He told me. Once, at their house, when I went to drop Brit off. Got her settled in, and he was there in the living room. He was drunk. Don't think he would've told me otherwise." A pause. "We shouldn't tell her, I figured. Probably best to let him tell her. Or to let her believe what she believes. Maybe it's better that way, sometimes."

I nodded.

# fifty-six

Mrs. Benson from the booster club came through my line at Safeway a few days later. The booster club was set to meet the week before school started, to review the summer's efforts and get a start on fall's fundraising agenda.

"Do you think we're still really far off from our target?" I said, ringing up her four, five, six boxes of instant oatmeal.

"Mm." Mrs. Benson fussed with her wallet, looking for her card. "We'll be okay." She located it, stuck it in the reader. "We actually—well, I probably should keep it under wraps, but you're head of the student group, so you get the inside scoop." She leaned in, eyes shining. "We got an anonymous donor who agreed to cover whatever we can't raise ourselves by the end of November."

My heart leaped. "So we'll be funded no matter what?"

She smiled. "You got it."

* * *

"Who knew?" Brit said after work. We were sitting around Flora's backyard with August. "Your Megan Pleasant scheme actually worked."

"What do you mean?"

"She's never going to come back here, but this way, she did her part for her town and can feel good about herself." Brit looked over. "I mean, obviously. Who else can give money like that?"

I glanced at August.

"I don't know what you're talking about," Heather said when we asked.

August shook his head. "I know you said you don't care about the money but you shouldn't do this, you should save it for Cady and Harper—"

"It's too much," I added.

"Megan did hear about the fall festival thing, you know," Heather said. "She told me her publicist or someone forwarded her a message about it. From a girl in Acadia, who wanted to get Megan's attention for her friend. Said it reminded her of us, way back when."

"It wasn't Megan who donated, though," I said.

She shrugged. "Maybe. You said it was anonymous."

"Heather."

A smile. "Maybe whoever it was is super confident in your fundraising abilities," she replied. "Maybe it won't be very much money at all."

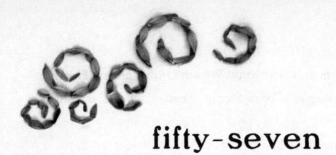

# fifty-seven

Brit and I were waiting around before band practice a few days later, sitting on the low wall outside the front of the school. The others weren't here yet, so Brit scrolled through her phone, and I leafed through the sheet music to "Reach Out."

And then I remembered what Heather had told us about Megan.

"Hey, you know what Heather said?"

"What?"

"Megan actually got one of our messages. She heard about the fall festival. Said it was from a girl who wrote on behalf of her friend."

"Huh."

She didn't look up from her phone.

I poked her shoulder. "What did you write?"

She made a face. "It was probably one of your messages. You sent her like a million."

"I never talked about one friend specifically. I only talked about the band in general."

Brit shook her head. "I didn't write her."

"Brit."

"I don't know a Megan Pleasant."

"Brittany Carter."

She made a face. "It wasn't much. Just . . . about you. And band. And how it was important to you, and how you're important to me, and stupid stuff like that, whatever, can we go inside now?"

"Did you send it through Megan Wants to Hear from You?"

She gave me an odd look. "No, I contacted her agency, who contacted her publicist."

"Why did that never come up in one single brainstorming session? Why didn't you have us all do that?"

"I don't know! I thought I'd give it a try! No one ever answered. I didn't think it went anywhere. Or that Megan cared about that kind of stuff anyway."

"Of course she does. Megan loves her fans more than anything."

"No." Brit shook her head and turned to me. "No, Sophie. For real. Look at me for a sec, because I just . . . need you to understand." I looked over at her. "Megan Pleasant is just a person. A regular person who feels and thinks and sleeps and has diarrhea sometimes, and probably hates some parts of her job, and likes other parts, and in the end, if she's smart, she loves herself more than anything."

"She—"

"I'm not saying it's a bad thing. I think it's . . . the best thing, actually. We should all love ourselves more than anything. You should put yourself before everything else, because in the end, you're the only person you've got, right? You're the only one you can really depend on."

I shook my head. "I'm always gonna put the people I love first. Always."

"I know that," she said. "I know. I hate that about you."

"Opposites," I murmured.

"You make these, like, *declarations* and you believe them. God, you talk about Flora, but it's you who thinks that everyone is as good as you are, everyone's willing to give as much, and I just . . . I don't want you to be disappointed by anyone ever."

I wouldn't say I worried about Flora. But I think Brit wouldn't say she worried about me either. It was probably the same sort of feeling.

Right now she frowned out at the parking lot, and when she spoke, it was gruff: "I don't want you to be disappointed by me ever."

I didn't know what to say, so I just knocked my shoulder against hers, and we both watched as Flora and Terrance approached from across the parking lot.

They were still a little ways away when Flora stopped. She gestured Terrance to her, put one hand up and braced herself on

Terrance's shoulder while she adjusted her shoe. She nearly tipped off center—he had to reach out and grab her. Her laugh rang out, a loud delighted peal.

Brit's gaze lingered on Flora, and the look on her face was one that I had never seen before. It was soft, and fond, and I flashed suddenly on Ravi, looking at Ciara as she held up two ice cream cones, grinning broadly. *Those look great*, he said, reaching for one. *I know*, she replied. *That's why they're both for me.*

I almost said "Oh" aloud, but caught myself. *Oh.*

Maybe I wasn't as smart as I thought I was. Or maybe I didn't know the people around me as well as I thought I did. Or maybe—maybe, maybe—the people around me were more than I was capable of imagining, contained more to them than I could fathom. Everyone had little pieces they kept to themselves, the same way I listed my schools, or reread my text messages—I knew that deep down. But somehow, you feel like you're the only one who's got undiscovered parts, when it's your best friends in the whole world in question. You feel like you must be the only one holding something back, when you knew someone as intrinsically as I knew Brit.

And yet.

She looked over at me. "Should we head in?"

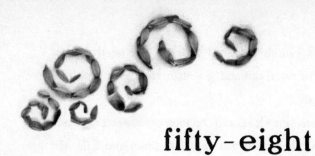

# fifty-eight

My phone buzzed that night. I had been in the middle of a text conversation with August about a new book I picked up at Bygones. It was by the same author as the previous one—*Summer Burn*—and I told August I was going to text it to him line by line.

But when I checked my phone, though, it wasn't August with another—

*PLEASE STOP*

*(don't stop)*

Instead, it was a series of texts from a different number:

*Have been growing it for a while*

*Finally went in for a cut and just had to make them pause halfway*

Then three pictures popped up—the back view of longish hair, thick and wet, combed straight. Then the side view, cut short on top. Then Ravi's face, his hair close-cropped in the front but hanging down on his shoulders. He was grinning, wide and silly, throwing up a peace sign.

*Business in the front, party in the back*, the next message read.

A burst of sound punched from me, equal parts laughter and sob.

*Amazing*, I replied.

# fifty-nine

I went to August's house the next day. We sat in the kitchen with the remainder of a cobbler that Heather's mom had made, eating it right out of the tin.

"Decent crust-to-fruit ratio," I said. "People never put enough crust on top, and that's the best part."

"What's a good percentage of crust?"

"At least fifty."

"Fifty percent crust? It's just cake, then. Upside-down cake with jam on it."

"Crust is not cake."

"Upside-down toast."

"Crust is not bread!"

"I'm sorry, is this your crust seminar?"

"Yes. I'm writing a dissertation on it. I'm about to get my crust PhD."

"Doctor Kemper," he said, raising an eyebrow. "Sounds good."

I smiled.

"Maybe I'll get one." I speared a blueberry with my fork. "A PhD. My sister wanted to go to grad school. She was studying biology. Wanted to do research and stuff."

"Yeah?"

"Mm." I squished the blueberry, watched the juice run out, and then I just said it, the thing I felt all the time, all the way down to my bones, to the marrow of them: "I wish she were here."

*She is*, people would say. *She's smiling down at you. She'll be with you every step of the way.*

*Yes*, I always wanted to reply. *Yes, maybe.* But that is nowhere near the same. It is in exactly no way the same as actually *being*.

August didn't say any of those things, though. He just nodded and scooted a bit of crust my way.

I took one last bite, set my fork down.

"Full?" he said.

"Cobbler full. We should eat something real."

I stood, went over to the pantry.

"I think there's leftover chili?" he said.

"How about I make us some mac and cheese?" I pulled a box out of the cabinet and presented it with a flourish. "The stove kind."

"The good stuff," August said.

301

"Yup." I started shaking the box like a maraca, dancing toward him. "Because I care," I said with a grin. "So, so, so, so much."

He grabbed me by the waist when I was close enough, grinning back, and we kissed until Shepherd's barking heralded the opening of the front door.

"We're home!"

"Mama said we'd come in the front door to give you fair warning!" Cadence called jubilantly.

We split apart, August smiling up at me as Cadence rounded the corner into the kitchen.

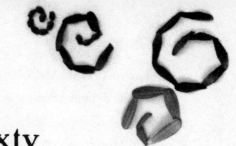

# sixty

**Sophie:**

I SAW ONE!!!!!!

**Ciara:**

NO WAY

**Sophie:**

At the gas station! FULL MULLET!

**Ciara:**

JLKSDFKLJSDFLKJ:SDFKLSDFKL

**Sophie:**

It was amazing. I feel like a new person

**Ciara:**

You should. That's a life changing haircut

**Sophie:**

Mom didn't super appreciate it though

Like she did but I don't think she really ~~~got~~~ it

Like this is a BIG DEAL

I wanted to take a pic to send you but she said no

**Ciara:**

Probably okay. Don't want to offend Mr. Mullet

Or Ms. Mullet?

Whatever their identity, a righteous mullet

**Sophie:**

Yes def

I wish you were here though

**Ciara:**

Me too. Christmas break!!!!!

**Sophie:**

FA LA LA LA LA

🌲🌲🌲🌲🌲🌲🌲🌲🌲🌲

**Ciara:**

🌲🌲🌲🌲🌲🌲🌲🌲🌲🌲🌲🌲🌲

🌲🌲🌲🌲🌲🌲🌲🌲🌲🌲🌲🌲🌲🌲🌲

🌲🌲🌲🌲🌲🌲🌲🌲🌲🌲🌲🌲🌲🌲🌲🌲🌲

**Sophie:**

OKAY ENOUGH TREES I REGRET IT

**Ciara:**

Fine bahahaha

## Sophie:
## JK I REGRET NOTHING

🌲🌲🌲🌲🌲🌲🌲🌲🌲🌲🌲🌲🌲🌲🌲🌲
🌲🌲🌲🌲🌲🌲🌲🌲🌲🌲🌲🌲🌲🌲🌲🌲

"Soph?"

"Hm?" I looked up from my phone, closing out of the message thread with Ciara. I had reached the end, but soon I would scroll back to the beginning and read them all again. And again.

"You ready?" Terrance smiled at me.

"For all of that?"

"For the last night of the summer," he said, and then he struck a pose. "And yes, also, all of this."

I smiled back. "I am a hundred and ten percent ready."

Dash and Terrance's dad grilled a bunch of stuff for us, and we ate out on the back deck. It was still bright out, but summer-night bright, where there's that evening slant to the light, the shadows going long.

Brit and August reached for the last brat at the same time. Brit waved a hand. "Go for it."

August speared it with his fork and transferred it to his plate.

"August Middle Name Shaw, I'm appalled," Brit said. "You're supposed to offer it to me too and then I get to refuse it again and feel like the better person. And anyway, I need the protein more than you."

He smiled, cutting the brat and dropping half on Brit's plate. "August is actually my middle name."

305

"What's your first name?" Terrance said.

"Christopher."

"Christopher August," Brit repeated immediately. "Christopher. Huh." A slow smile took her face. "What if we called you Topher?"

"Please don't."

"No, but like, what if you had gone by Toph instead? What would your life have been like?"

Flora's eyes brightened. "That's your Other Acadia name! You're Toph in Other Acadia!"

"Toph drives a Volvo."

"Nah." Dash shook his head. "No way. Toph drives a used Range Rover."

"Toph plays lacrosse. Second string but he thinks he has a *really good* shot at starting this year," Terrance said.

Brit took a large bite of brat and, with her mouth full, contributed: "Toph almost got to third base on the sectional in his girlfriend's stepdad's basement the night of homecoming junior year, but the stepdad came home early and the girlfriend made him climb out the basement window."

Terrance nodded. "He tore his tux pants on the window casing and he got charged for it at the rental place. He and the girlfriend broke up two weeks later for unrelated reasons."

"This shit is weirdly specific, guys," August said.

"Toph thinks he's allergic to citrus fruits."

"Toph puts sriracha on *everything.*"

"If I ever met Toph, I would punch him," Brit said.

"You'd have to get in line," August replied.

"Toph is doing his best," Flora said. "I like him."

Brit gasped. "Flora is Toph's Other Acadia girlfriend!"

"No, I'm not!"

Terrance gasped too. "You broke up with him after the rental-tux incident!"

"Nooo!" August clutched his chest. "You said it was unrelated!"

Flora extended a hand to me across the table. "You can date August in Other Acadia too, Sophie."

"Oh gee, may I?"

"I am feeling *awfully* attacked right now," August said.

"Welcome to the group," Brit replied with a grin.

Brit and I sat on the deck steps after dinner, while Flora and the guys threw a ball around. August was stationed in one of the plastic chairs from Teen Zone 2, trying valiantly not to pitch backward as he reached for one-handed catches. He managed to stay upright but had missed all of them so far.

"So is it official?" I said. "Are we adding August to the chat?"

"On a trial basis," she replied. "He posts one bad meme, he's out."

"Who decides what's a good meme and bad meme?"

"Me, obviously."

"Oh, obviously."

Brit smiled.

It was the same kind of smile she would eventually shoot me that autumn when Chelsea Peters reprised her ukulele rendition of

"Steel Highway" at the fall festival's Megan Pleasant contest. Megan wouldn't be in attendance. Chelsea wouldn't win, either, but both outcomes were okay.

We wouldn't entirely fill in the Rose Parade fundraising thermometer by November, but we'd be close. With the various efforts of the booster committee, the anonymous donor's contribution wouldn't be huge.

Pasadena would be beautiful. The "Sounds of the '60s" medley would be a hit, and my mom would proudly post screenshots from the two and a half seconds when you could see me in a wide shot on the TV broadcast.

August wouldn't end up joining band. But he'd send me a picture of Cady and Harper sitting in front of the television, watching the parade. He would share the screenshots my mom posted, adding an embarrassing number of emojis and exclamation points. When we got back to Acadia, he'd ask all about it, every step of the way, even though I had been updating him throughout.

*It's different hearing it in person.*

*How's that?*

*I can do this,* he'd say, and kiss me.

*Yeah, but, like, don't do that too often, or I'll never get through it all,* I'd reply with a grin.

It would always be easy to lose track of time when I was kissing him.

He would visit his mom, eventually. With Kyle, and without him. With me too.

But right now, in the Cunninghams' backyard, all of that was unknown. Right now, Brit just looked at me, eyes shining as she said, "I have a question for you."

"Go for it."

She leaned in, dropping down to a whisper: "Where will you spend eternity?"

I grinned up at the sky, the sun dipping below the trees.

"I don't know where, but I know how."

"Hm?"

"How I'll spend it."

"And how's that?"

"Loving you guys," I said, taking her hand and giving it a squeeze.

"I hate that you said that," Brit murmured, and squeezed back.

# acknowledgments

I have been so fortunate to work with a group of passionate and enthusiastic individuals to bring this book to life. Many, many thanks to Bridget Smith, agent prime, and Kate Farrell, all-time editor. Thank you to the talented folks at Macmillan/Henry Holt, in particular the sunny and ever-efficient Rachel Murray, powerhouse publicist Brittany Pearlman, and the excellent Fierce Reads team. Thank you to Liz Dresner and Becca Clason for the absolutely gorgeous cover design and artwork.

Mama and Papa deserve particular recognition for helping me through this one—it was no easy task, and I am very grateful! Additional thanks to Hannie and Cap-Cap, for demonstrating a relationship founded on love and pre-determined boomerang ownership. To Pei-Ciao, Jiyoon, Rachel, Shawn, Eshaani, and Lakshmi, for being amazing friends. To Rochelle, for the thoughtful read-through and critique. To Wintaye, for always being down for book discussions. To my lab-mates old and new, who have helped me immeasurably over the last five years of PhD study. To Mike, for discussing your marching band days with me back in our How to Adult days! Becky, technically you were already acknowledged, but thank you anyway, for being there for me ever since we both had bangs.

To all of you who have read, shared, blogged, reviewed, tweeted, tumbled, or otherwise engaged with my books, thank you thank you thank you! To librarians and booksellers, you are pillars of this industry, and I can't thank you enough for all that you do.

I have driven I-70 through Illinois many, many times in the past few years, and this book was born in part from towns along the way. In particular, Pocahontas, Greenville, Vandalia, and Casey—thank you for the inspiration. And thanks of course to my very favorite small town of all: the one I grew up in!